A Taste of Love: Richard

Published by Phaze Books
Also by Marie Rochelle

All the Fixin'

My Deepest Love: Zack

Caught

Loving True

Taken By Storm

Cincinnati, Ohio

www.Phaze.com

A Taste of Love: Richard

A novel of erotic romance by

MARIE ROCHELLE

Cincinnati, Ohio

A Phaze Production
Phaze Books
6470A Glenway Avenue, #109
Cincinnati, OH 45211-5222
Phaze is an imprint of Mundania Press, LLC.

To order additional copies of this book, contact:
books@phaze.com
www.Phaze.com

Cover art © 2008 Debi Lewis
Edited by Amanda Faith

Trade Paperback ISBN-13: 978-1-60659-085-0
First Print Edition – October, 2008
Printed in the United States of America

10 9 8 7 6 5 4 3 2 1

Dedication

To Dee Dee.

I can't believe you're gone.

Thanks so much for being like a second grandmother to me.

Chapter One

"What are we going to do about the chaos going on out there?" the waiter asked his boss, who was seated behind the desk in front of him. The dark-haired man opened a bottle of pain relievers and tossed back two, followed by a large gulp of coffee.

"Steve, just go back out there and try to settle everyone down," Richard Drace told his new employee in the nicest voice he could muster.

"Sir, it's going to take more than a free meal to please the livid man at table six," Steve exclaimed. "He wants to speak with the manager," he emphasized with a wave of his thin, bony hand.

Richard jumped up from his seat so fast that the chair rolled back and crashed against the wall. "Tell him he doesn't get everything he wants, and if he isn't happy with the service at D4, maybe he needs to leave," he snapped.

"Okay, I'll do that," Steve said before he raced out of the room, closing the door quickly behind him.

Falling back down into the leather seat, Richard couldn't believe how out of hand his life had become in the last six months, and it was entirely his fault. Why did he hire another employee when it couldn't afford to pay the eight he already had?

"Shit," he groaned under his breath, worried about the future of his business.

Of course, he knew the reason for his problems, like everyone else who was outside that door. He wanted to prove he could do the job as well as *she* had. Yet, the books hadn't been the same since she walked out of this very office with a box in her hand. It would have only taken two minutes for him to run after her and whisper the words he had been thinking about for months now.

He dropped his head to the desk, and it landed with a loud thump. It almost blocked out the noise coming through the door. "Can't I get a moment's peace?" Richard mumbled inside the empty room. "It never sounded like this when she was here."

The sounds of dishes breaking in the kitchen that he couldn't keep filled with food sent him flying out the door. "What in the world are you doing in here? Those dishes are expensive, and I can't afford for one to get broken. Damn it! Watch what you're doing!" he yelled, gaze swinging back and forth over his nervous crew.

"Mr. Drace, it was only one dish," Steve answered, tossing the plate into the trashcan by the sink.

"All of you came whining to me, asking for your jobs back, and I gave them back to you. However, I lost the best manager I had in the process. So, Steve, it's more than one dish. I'm slowly losing my business because of all of the chaos that goes on in this kitchen. None of you are carrying your weight, and it's beginning to overflow to the customers and the service they're receiving."

"I don't think all the blame should be put on us," Melissa, another employee, chimed in. "We do a lot here. I don't know how you can ask me to do anymore. All of us already give you more than a hundred percent of our time."

Richard bit back his quick comment and slowly addressed his employees. "Now, we all are going to pitch in by doing extra jobs or working longer hours, making it over a hundred percent," he remarked, taking a look in Melissa's direction. "Starting now, we don't have any personal lives outside these doors. If I say you have to work an extra shift, it will get done without a complaint, or you can quit and I'll replace you with someone who wants the job." His voice held an edge of warning. He wanted his staff to realize that they might have gotten rid of the wrong person. "I'm going out for a while, and when I come back, I want this kitchen clean and my customers happy."

Storming away from the group, Richard walked out into the dining area of his dream and noticed how empty the restaurant was now. Customers had stopped coming in like they used to when Dawn was the manager. *D4* had only been open six months, and he was already having money problems. His brother Lee had offered him a loan, and so had Zack, but he had declined both offers.

For once in his adult life, he was tired of being the brother who couldn't make any of his plans work out long-term. Owning his own business had always been a dream of his, and now it might have to end if *D4* didn't pick up any more business than this.

His pride had cost him the brilliant Dawn Summers. For the few weeks she had been the manager here, the place had been overflowed with customers and word of mouth had been hot. In the back of his mind, he thought most of the male customers came to get a look at how beautiful she was.

She had a way of making everyone feel welcome as soon as they walked in the door and got seated. More than one person had asked where she had gone, and after he told them, they had left without even ordering a meal.

Daily his business continued to go down the drain, and he didn't know how to stop it. If he lost any more money, *D4* would be just a memory in Houston. Without saying a word to the crew, Richard hurried out of the building, shoving his hands into his pockets, deciding on what to do.

* * * *

Spreading out the newspaper on the picnic table, Dawn pulled the red Sharpie pen out of her handbag and searched for another job. Her eyes dropped down to the want ads and skimmed over them. "I can't stand one more day at that place," she complained as a bird sang above her in a tree. "Why did I even say yes?" *Because I have bills to pay and an empty checking account won't help me with rent, water, or cable*, she thought.

Biting into the apple, she prayed she would spot another restaurant manager's job, so her four-year business degree wouldn't be wasted. Thinking about her old manager's job brought Richard Drace front and center in her mind. "Stop thinking about that man after what he did to you," she scolded herself, tossing the apple into the trashcan beside her. "He didn't want you in his life or business, so why are you still giving him a second thought?"

Yet, his compelling, magnetic eyes were rooted in her mind like a bad dream. All she had to do was close her eyes, and there they were, staring back. "Richard Drace is one man who's way out of your league." *D4* had been in the papers a lot lately. She remembered reading a critic's comments just last week, wondering how a business started out with such promise only to slowly fade into the background.

Several times she had wanted to go back and offer Richard some help, but the last instance they had been together was different from any other time. He had pressed her back against the wall with his tall, towering body and leaned down like he was going to kiss her until Melissa burst in on them. Ashamed at being caught in that position with him, Dawn shoved Richard away and then rushed from the office.

Deep down, the love she felt for Richard was still there, waiting to be stoked by him. But Richard wasn't interested in her like that and never would be. It had pained her seeing him out with Emily two nights ago. Swallowing down the hurt at the memory, Dawn looked back down at the newspaper in front of her. "Get over him and move on. Once I have enough money saved up, I can get out of this town."

* * * *

Walking with his head down, lost in his own personal thoughts, Richard didn't see Dawn sitting at the bench until he was almost upon her beautiful form. The afternoon sunlight bounced off her shoulder-length black hair that now had a kinkier look to it. She was just as he recalled—gorgeous. Moving softly so he wouldn't startle her, Richard stopped in front of the table, blocking out the sun.

"Hello, Dawn."

Dawn looked up and gasped when she found him standing above her. "What are you doing here?"

"Can I join you?" he asked, pointing to the empty seat. It was fate. He was meant to leave D4 to find her.

"Sure," she replied, sliding the newspaper closer to her.

A smile touched the side of his mouth as he slid in front of her and noticed the want ads. "Are you looking for a job?" Richard drawled with the Texas accent he knew Dawn loved so much.

"Girl has to pay bills," she answered, looking at him quickly and then back down at the newspaper.

Closing his eyes, Richard said a quick thanks and reopened them. He took the paper away from Dawn and pitched it into the trash. "I have the perfect job for you."

"Hey, don't do that," she snapped, getting up, reaching towards the paper.

Richard touched Dawn's arm, noticing how soft her skin was. "Please sit back down so we can talk," he said softly. Her eyes filled with suspicion as Dawn did as he asked.

"Would you think about coming back to D4 as manager?" his silky voice asked.

Her eyes widened in shock, as Dawn drew back from him in amazement. "Y-you can't be serious?" she stammered.

Leaning forward on the bench, he said in a controlled voice, "I wouldn't joke about my business. I know you read the papers and saw that *D4* is in a lot of trouble. I know you can help me get it back on top."

Jumping up from the picnic table, Dawn grabbed her purse without answering him and headed back to her car in the parking lot. She had moved so fast that Richard sat there, stunned, before it dawned on him to get up and follow her.

"Stop!" he yelled, chasing after Dawn. Catching her at the grass's edge, he spun her back around to face him. "Did you not enjoy working with me?" he questioned.

"It was okay," she replied, shaking off his touch. Moving to her car, she unlocked it and got in without taking another look in his direction.

"Please reconsider coming back," Richard pleaded as Dawn was closing the door. "I need you," he pleaded, stepping back from the car as she pulled out. Richard hoped he had reached the soft spot that he knew was inside Dawn.

* * * *

When Richard got back to the restaurant, there wasn't a customer in sight, and the crew was in the back, cleaning up the kitchen. "Everyone can stop working and go home," he told his employees. Everyone stopped working and stared at him like he had spoken a foreign language.

"Are you saying we're fired?" Melissa asked.

"I can't afford to keep paying you and save *D4* at the same time." Richard replied, looking at his stunned workers. "So I'm going to let you go and close down for a while. Hopefully, I can hire another manager or, if I'm lucky, get Dawn to come back." He heard the groans coming from Melissa. "If you have a problem with Miss Summers, you can leave now because I have spoken with her and offered her the position back."

He wasn't going to be dumb and allow Melissa or anyone else to cost him Dawn again if she came back to work for him. While she was gone, he had started to realize that he wanted a little more than an employer and employee relationship with his stunning former manager.

"I've your paychecks back in the office if you come with me. I'll pass them out," Richard stated, going toward the back of the building. He paid his staff and thanked them for their service. All of them but one filed out of his office in a state of confusion, and he could understand why. Melissa stayed behind and gave him a harsh look. He didn't need three guesses to know what her problem was.

"Do you really want to bring Dawn back?" she complained, standing at the edge of his desk. "She had such horrible people skills. I don't know if I can come back here if she comes back as manager."

Richard knew now that Dawn was right about Melissa and he should have never hired her back. The way she lingered behind him and gave him her advice was something he didn't appreciate.

"Melissa, you don't have any say if Dawn comes back as manager or not. You're my employee, not my business partner. I think it would be best if you took your check and left," he said, holding it out to her between two fingers.

Snatching the check out of his hand, Melissa stormed towards the door. "Well, I can promise you that I won't be back if Dawn is rehired. I can't work for someone like her." With that, she marched out of the room.

Reclining in the desk chair, he looked around the small, cramped space that he called his office. *D4* was the most important thing in his life right now. Dawn had to come back to help him save it. Seeing her today in the park had been a sign she was meant to be in his life. It had been almost two months to the day since she walked out of this office.

Richard couldn't believe how touching her today affected his blood pressure. It had shot up to a dangerous level. He wondered what made Dawn want to leave her current job. The last time he had heard about her, she had a good job working for a firm. Hell, he didn't care about the reason as long as he could convince her to come back. Pulling a legal pad from his desk, Richard started writing down ideas for how to save his business.

* * * *

"How long do you want me to work for you?" Dawn's voice broke through Richard's thoughts as she came into his office.

He wanted to be surprised to see her, but he wasn't. He knew that Dawn loved the time she spent here at *D4*. Sitting up straighter, his gaze slowly traveled up her body, finally making eye contact. He couldn't stop the pleasure he felt from shining through.

"I can't say, because I don't know how long it will take you to save my restaurant," he confessed.

Thank God, she's going to take the offer. Stay calm and don't scare her away.

"What went wrong after I left?" Dawn asked.

"Do you mind having a seat so we can talk better?" he asked, pointing to a seat in front of her.

Coming further into his office, Dawn sat down on the edge of the chair and stared at him. Richard saw the uneasiness on her face and the distrust in her eyes. He hated that he put that look on her face, but he would try his damnedest to get rid of it. "I'm really glad you decided to take my offer." Richard smiled, lighting up his already handsome face.

Dawn kept herself calm. "I should let you know that when *D4* is back up and running the way you want it, I will leave," she tossed out, shocking him. "Too many of the employees don't like how I run the business, but I can't allow a place as beautiful as this to fail."

Looking at her mouth, Richard wondered what it would be like to kiss her. Dawn looked so striking in her lavender top and matching skirt. They brought out the richness of her lovely brown skin. Focusing back on the words coming out of her luscious mouth was hard, but he did it. "Dawn, I fired the staff. If you want to hire all new employees, we can. I'm a hundred percent behind you this time," he stated, staring straight into her eyes. "I want to you know that I'm willing to do anything to help you."

Dawn didn't seem to trust how agreeable Richard was being with her. "I don't understand the change in you. The last time we talked about this, you let me know I was just the manager and nothing else. Did you wake up one day and change your mind?" she asked, arching one eyebrow over soulful eyes.

Chuckling, Richard loved that Dawn still had the outspokenness he found so sexy. "Can't I admit to being wrong without you rubbing it in more? I know you were the one who kept the suppliers and investors happy when I wasn't around to do it. You wouldn't believe how many of them told me I needed to hire you back."

Folding his hands, he placed them on the desk, leaning forward to be a little closer to her. "Dawn, I think you have your own mini-fan club," he teased, making his drawl more noticeable. "How did it get past me how much they liked you?" he asked, flashing a sexy smile.

Crossing her unbelievable legs, Dawn adjusted her skirt before answering him. "You were busy with your girlfriend Emily, and then you had to keep Melissa happy so she wouldn't quit. Other things were more important to you at that critical time, and I took on the problems of D4. Isn't that what a good manager does when the owner is MIA?"

Pissed off by the way Dawn pointed out his flaws, Richard wanted to hurt her back. "The reason I stopped coming around was much as I should have was I got tired of you constantly having a crush on me."

Dawn took his insult without batting an eye. "I guess we both know where we stand with each other. If you don't have anything else to say, I'd like my job back."

Richard wanted to take the words back. Dawn didn't have to come back, but she was doing it.

Clearing his throat, he said, "I should apologize for what I just said." He watched her face for a reaction.

"Why should you apologize when you meant every word? Your honesty is what I like the best about you. Don't change it now," Dawn retorted. "The only thing I wanted to add to my agreement is that you'll give me a good reference when I leave."

"I can't believe you're serious about that," Richard said, confused, as he got up and moved within touching distance of Dawn. "You're really going to leave after you help me? What if I want to hire you permanently?"

Dawn shook her head. "I can't agree to that. Like I said earlier, I'll help you get *D4* back up and running, but after that, I'm leaving Houston and would appreciate a reference from you," she informed him staring straight into his eyes.

Perched on the edge of the seat, she waited for an answer. Words left Richard at the possibility of Dawn no longer being in the same town. He would agree to her wishes for now because, in the end, Dawn wouldn't leave him or the restaurant. "You have a deal, Miss Summers," he said.

Following his movements, Dawn stood up and shook his hand. "Good. I'll see you tomorrow morning at eight o'clock sharp."

"Why can't we get started right now?" he asked, shocked by the fact that Dawn was leaving.

"I've a date," she replied, going out the door without looking back.

Richard didn't like being jealous, but he was. Dawn didn't need any distractions from him or the restaurant. He needed her free for any time he might want her. *Oh, you want her and not at only to help with D4.* Tomorrow, they would set some ground rules about dating while helping him out. There would be no outside dating until *D4* was up and running smoothly again. The only man she was going to be spending any time with was him.

Instead of following Dawn and finding out who her date was, Richard decided to stay at *D4*. He had to make sure all the windows and doors were locked and the security alarm was set. Richard wondered who Dawn had a date with, because during the two months she had worked for him, he never saw a guy around her.

Why did he care so much anyway? Dawn only wanted to be his employee now and nothing else. So why couldn't he forget how so soft her skin felt hours ago, or how her perfume still lingered in the room? Yet he did notice how Dawn didn't look at him like she used to, and it did hurt a little.

Richard knew he needed a night out to push Dawn to the back of his mind. Until he came to grips with the fact it might be too late and he might have already lost her to another man, Emily was always happy to hear from him. He would drop by her house on his way home. If Dawn had a date tonight, he sure in the hell was going to have one, too. Even if it wasn't with the woman he wanted.

* * * *

"I'm so happy you came by," Emily said, handing him a brandy. "I've been thinking about you. Did Zack tell you I asked how you were doing?" Emily asked, placing her hand on his thigh as she joined him back on the couch.

Richard glanced down at Emily's hand and the blatant invitation she was giving him, but tonight, like every other time, he wasn't interested in sleeping with her. Removing her hand, he laid it on the seat between them. "How are things going at work for you? Are you still up for the promotion?" he inquired, trying to show some interest in her life. Yet his mind was on Dawn and her mystery date. What were they doing at this exact moment? Where they kissing or, worse, making love?

As much as he hated it, Richard gave his attention back to Emily and flinched as she lit a cigarette, took a long puff, and blew it out before answering. Coughing, he gave Emily a long look. "Do you mind putting that out? You know how much I hate it when you smoke."

Emily got rid of the cigarette while blowing the rest of the smoke out of the side of her mouth. "Sorry, I forgot you aren't a smoker."

"Please try to remember next time," he suggested, placing his drink on the table as he tried to think of a reason he wanted to stay.

"I don't know about the promotion yet. I might hear something by the end of the week." Fixing her hair, she slid closer to him on the couch, touching him lightly on the arm.

"Baby, have you decided what you're going to do about your business? I could help you," she suggested, touching the back of his hand. "I know a lot of people who are always looking for a good investment."

Richard removed Emily's hand from his. "I'm getting some help from a friend," he told her, bored.

God, why did he keep coming back here? Emily talked nonstop, and he forgot how much it drove him up the wall. He needed to be home figuring out a way to win Dawn back.

"Do I know this friend?" she asked.

He didn't have time for Emily's attempt at sneaking information from him. This had been a bad idea, coming over here, because it was always the same. Emily would try to seduce him into her bed, and he would tell her no. When would he learn to stop making the same mistake?

"Yes, you do know this person," he said, standing up to leave.

Emily jumped up with him. "Oh, you don't have to leave so soon." She pouted, trying to make him stay.

"I'm afraid that I do," he said, going to the door, needing to get away from Emily's whining voice. It was too much for him to take this late at night. Dawn would be on time tomorrow, and he wanted to be at D4 before she got there. He strolled across Emily's beige carpet and opened the front door.

"Are you going to tell me who the friend is?" Emily asked as he went through the open door.

"Dawn," he yelled back, closing the door with a loud click.

Chapter Two

Standing outside Richard's office door the next morning at eight o'clock sharp, Dawn willed herself to stay calm in his presence. He had a way of making her go weak in the knees with that heavy stare and deep drawl of his. In the past, she would ask him questions just to hear him talk, but it was different now. Richard didn't want her attention and made it known by the way he spoke to her yesterday.

This was only business with her; he was in love with Emily and didn't want her crush on him. No matter how sexy her boss was, it wouldn't stop her from working shoulder to shoulder with him to save D4.

Raising her hand, she knocked once on the door and then waited for an answer. She had no clue in what direction this day was going, but she knew she wasn't going to show Richard she still had feelings for him. He would never see her in the same light as she saw him.

"Enter," Richard's perfect voice yelled from the other side of the door.

Taking a relaxing, deep breath, Dawn turned the doorknob, walked into the office, and almost fell over at the delicious sight of Richard standing in the middle of the floor. The sight of him caused her mouth to drop open. He was standing there with his shirt wide open, running a towel through his damp hair. His chest hair went from his collarbone all the way down to into his snug-fitting jeans that were pulled over cowboy boots.

Dawn gripped the doorknob tighter so she wouldn't pass out or rush over and run her hands all over his body. "Did I catch you at a bad time?" she asked, looking into his eyes and not at his amazing chest.

"Damn pipe burst! My hair and shirt got wet when I was turning it off," Richard hissed, removing the towel from his hair and tossing it in the chair. Picking up another one, he ran it up and down his chest while looking at the expression on Dawn's face. She was shocked as hell to see him standing half-naked in front of her.

Leaving the shirt open, Richard tossed the other towel next to the first one. "Close the door and have a seat, Dawn." He pointed to a small table on the far side of the room. He walked over there and waited for her to join him.

"Sure," Dawn said, shutting the door and then coming toward him.

Richard's eyes followed the movement of Dawn's legs in the heels, as though enjoying how they made her shorter legs look longer. The short tan skirt with slit at the side showcased shapely thighs, and the snug white top flattered her two best assets.

Pulling out the chair, Dawn moved it away from him and then took a seat, trying her best to ignore him. However, she prayed he didn't notice how her eyes kept glancing at his damp chest. Hell, she was a woman, and Richard was a good-looking man. How could she not stare at him?

"Tell me where you want to begin," he whispered by her ear, sending shivers up and down her body. "I'm all yours for as long as want me."

Moving her head slightly, Dawn looked directly into Richard's sea-green eyes, wondering was there a double meaning to what he just said. But as she stared at him, nothing showed in his eyes.

"Maybe the first thing we should do is set some work hours. So if either of us has other plans, we can work up until then and leave the rest for the next day," she suggested, pulling a pad out of the bag she brought with her.

"Like I said earlier, I'm all yours for any way you want to use me," he drawled again, his hot breath tickling her sensitive earlobe.

Shivering, Dawn made herself not look at Richard because if he was playing a game, she wasn't going to be a part of it. "Fine, then, I was thinking the hours should be from eight o'clock to four o'clock. With those hours, you'll have your nights free, and so will I," she said, writing down the information.

Leaning closer so his bare chest brushed her arm, Richard tapped the pad. "What if I want to work longer than that?" he asked, while the smell of his cologne slowly drove her crazy.

Dawn was proud that she didn't flinch when Richard's nose touched the side of her neck. He was driving her wild with his close body contact. Before, Richard never allowed his body to brush against hers all the time she had worked here. So what was up with the change in him now?

"I work for you, and that includes the hours you want," Dawn informed Richard, leaning away from his body. She could feel his chest hair through the sleeve of her thin shirt, and it was making her body scream.

"Good. I don't think either one of us should be dating until *D4* is back up and running the way I need it to be," he said, touching the back of her hand.

Slipping his arm around the back of her chair, Richard brought their mouths within kissing distance of each other. If she moved an inch, she would know what it would be like to kiss Richard. Did she want to know?

* * * *

Kiss her, kiss her, kiss her, you idiot, his mind screamed at him. Dawn's lips looked so moist and red; all he had to do was lean in. As Richard moved his head for the kiss, the office door swung open.

"Richard, I need to talk to you," Brad said, barging into the room, but he stopped in his tracks when he saw the two of them about to kiss. "Sorry, man. I didn't know Dawn was here," he said, trying to back out of the room.

Richard cursed under his breath as Dawn fell back in the chair. The shock of almost being caught kissing him was clear in her huge eyes. "Don't go now," he snapped at his younger brother. The moment was ruined, and Dawn looked like she was about to bolt from her seat.

"I need to check on a few things," Dawn said, getting up from the table with notepad in hand. "Hi, Brad," she said, hurrying out the door.

"Did I ever tell you what wonderful timing you have?" Richard growled, standing up and buttoning his shirt as Brad shut the door behind Dawn. He was glad his brother did that because he didn't want Dawn overhearing their conversation.

"I didn't believe Lee when he told me you had hired Dawn back," Brad said, nodding his head towards the closed door. "I thought you couldn't stand her. That's all you used to say at our weekly dinners."

"People's feelings can change," Richard commented, sitting behind his desk. "Tell me what brings you all the way here to ruin my life."

Brad flung his tall body down into the chair, running his fingers through his sun-bleached blond hair. "I've a problem," he muttered.

"Let me guess," Richard said. "Is her name Alicia Hart?"

"How did you know?" Brad asked, surprise clear in his voice.

"Man, Alicia has been driving you crazy for a while now. What has the hot little reporter done this time?"

Brad crossed one leg over the other, running his hands over the five o'clock shadow. "She wants to stop the tennis lessons because the guy she was trying to impress doesn't like tennis anymore. Hell, if she stops the lessons, I don't have any other excuse to be around her," Brad groaned.

"Aren't you friends with her? Why can't you just go out on a friendly date?" Richard questioned.

"Alicia doesn't know I'm in love with her," Brad confessed softly.

"Is she blind?" Richard asked, his eyebrow arching high on his forehead. The way his brother drooled all over her anytime she came into the room, she had to be on another planet not to see his feelings.

"Alicia has a hard time seeing what's right in her face, which I find really strange for a reporter, plus this Max keeps jerking her around," Brad complained. "One minute he wants to be with her, and the next he's dating another woman. Why is she allowing that to happen?" Brad asked. He rubbed the back of his neck. "So I decided to spend more time at the office with Lee, and he's about to drive me crazy."

Richard didn't know how to answer his brother's question. "Brad, some people don't know how to leave a situation. But if you really care about Alicia, don't give up on her," he encouraged. "And, well, you know Lee is crazy when it comes to work. You know how much he loves making money."

"Thanks for the advice. I want Alicia in my life and I need to find a way to make it happen," Brad mused.

"Hey, that's what big brothers are for," Richard answered, happy that Brad felt that he could come to him with his problems.

"Are you trying to get something going with Dawn?" Brad asked, changing to conversation back to him. "You looked pretty cozy. I wonder what would have happened if I hadn't walked in."

"Don't worry about Dawn and me," Richard muttered.

Brad knew by the tone of his brother's voice that he had overstayed his welcome. Getting up, he made his way to the door. "I have a suggestion for you," he whispered back at Richard.

"What is it?"

"Lock the door the next time you want to get busy with Dawn," Brad laughed as Richard threw a book at him before he closed the door.

Chapter Three

Sitting in a booth, Dawn waited until she saw Brad leave the office, then went back to have a talk with Richard. She couldn't figure out what kind of game he was playing, but it would stop or the business deal was over. Not bothering to knock, she stormed into the office. "What in the hell were you trying to do earlier?" she demanded, tossing her pad down on the desk.

Richard's green eyes stared at her. "I don't know what you're talking about," he replied innocently. Folding his hands behind the back of his neck, Richard rested his head in them and leaned back in his chair.

"Don't you dare lie to me, Richard," she snapped. "If Brad hadn't walked in, your tongue would have been in my mouth."

Dawn didn't miss the desire that flared up in her boss's eyes, but she refused to acknowledge it. She was beyond pissed at the hunk daring her to react to him. She needed this job, and Richard wasn't going to scare her away from it. He was enjoying teasing her.

"Is that what you wanted to happen, Dawn?" he asked in a heated voice.

Storming around the desk, Dawn poked her finger in Richard's rock-hard chest, trying not to notice how good it felt. "You need to keep all your body parts to yourself," she informed him, looking deeply into his eyes. "Find your release with someone else, not me."

She turned to leave, but Richard's hands shot out, jerking her back to his chest. "What happened last night, Dawn? Did your date not know how to perform?" he taunted in her ear.

Snatching her arm away, she raised her hand to slap him, but Richard caught her, toppling her back into the seat and into his chest. He covered her mouth quickly with his, and his tongue thrust deep in her mouth.

Holding her against him with one hand, Richard slid the other into Dawn's hair, tilting her head back to deepen the already hot kiss. Dawn tried to get away by shoving at his chest, but he wasn't budging.

Finally realizing she wasn't getting away until he was ready to let her go, she relaxed on his chest and let him kiss her. Feeling her submit caused him to break the white-hot kiss, and his eyes searched hers, then he withdrew his hands from her hair and waist.

Jumping up from his lap, Dawn hissed, "If you ever do that again, I'll walk out of here without a second thought." Picking up the pad from the table, she went over and retrieved her purse from the floor. "I'll see you tomorrow, and you better remember to keep your hands to yourself," she snapped, storming out the door.

* * * *

Stopping at a drive-thru, Dawn picked up some dinner and then headed home. Once there, she checked her answering machine, but there weren't any messages. Today hadn't turned out at all like she thought it would. Working with Richard was going to be harder than her mind ever thought. How could she work with him and be indifferent when her body was going to betray her at every turn?

Seeing him with his shirt open had almost been her downfall, but she got through it with flying colors. Then what did that green-eyed devil do? He kissed her. No, it wasn't a kiss, but a switching of souls. Richard's mouth showed her what a kiss was like when you're in love with the other person. However, she knew that her love was one-sided. Richard Drace wasn't in love with her and never would be.

The question was, why did he kiss her in the first place? He wasn't the kind of man to kiss a woman without a good reason. Were he and Emily having problems, so he needed to find a release? Well, shit. He wasn't going to use her as a part-time plaything. She meant what she said; if he pulled something like that again, she would leave him. It didn't matter how fine his ass was.

Oh, you know you aren't going anywhere until you have that business back up and running for him. You love D4 as much as you love the owner. "Hell, I'm trying my best not to love him, but it's so hard," Dawn said.

If Dawn hadn't gone to that out-of-town convention with one of her friends over two years ago to kill some time, she would have never seen Richard Drace, let alone fall in love with him. The amazing thing was Richard looked the same as he had when she spotted him at the conference. Next week would make three years to the day since she had seen him standing no less than twenty feet in front of her, talking to a group of men about starting up his business.

Richard had worn a dark blue suit with a tie, looking every bit the up-and-coming businessman that he wanted to be. Dawn knew the thing that had caught her attention first was his sexy, Texas drawl. Every word that came from his mouth made her blood sizzle in her veins. Not being the kind of woman who got instantly attracted to a man, and a stranger at that, she was blown away and had to think of a way to draw him into a conversation with her.

It never happened, and the only way she had learned anything about him was one of the speakers at the event had sat behind some people and started talking about him. Since that moment, Dawn had had a need to know more about the handsome Texan. So she left her job in Arizona as a restaurant manager and moved to Texas, hoping to become better aquainted with Richard. At the time, it didn't seem like she was acting in an irrational manner, but like a woman, she saw what she wanted and went after it.

For months, she worked odd jobs, waiting for him to open his restaurant D4, which was named for all his brothers. The waiting paid off in the end. Working with Richard was worth all the money and time and effort she had thrown into it. Going to work every day and seeing his face had brought a smile to hers, but he never felt the same way towards her. Richard thought she was pushy, stubborn, bossy, and power-hungry.

He told her to stay in her place as the manager and he would make any big decisions. God, she was so into him back then that she had allowed him to talk to her like that, but it all ended the day he hired Melissa. Melissa was the worst employee she had ever managed in her whole seven-year career. She was always showing up late and talking on the phone nonstop, but Dawn had drawn the line with how Melissa disrespected the customers time and time again.

Of course, she waited until after work late one night to talk to Melissa about her attitude. However, Melissa, being the way she was, just blew her off. After that conversation, she had gone to see Richard, and he didn't turn out to be much help, either. He wasn't listening to her about Melissa's rudeness towards the customers, but he told her the only reason she was complaining about Melissa was out of jealousy. At first, his comment threw her because she had never been envious of any other woman in her life.

To her, jealousy was a wasted emotion that she wasn't cursed with. If you were resentful of someone, you could take that extra energy and place it towards a more important project. Richard continued taunting her by saying she wanted the same attention he showered on the younger, sexier Melissa. Lastly, he ended with someone like her should know her place and stay in it.

Never had she been so insulted and pissed off in her life. She had boxed up what few personal items she owned and walked out the doors of *D4*. Oh, a few weeks later Richard had left a message on her answering machine asking her to come back, but the wounds were still too fresh, and she didn't do it.

Now, it was almost six months later and he had finally convinced her into coming back. However, this time they were going to play by her rules, not his. Richard wouldn't charm his way into her life or bed. It was totally business between them now.

Why should it matter that her heart still did a little flip-flop when his tall, lean frame sauntered into the room? Or how that sexy drawl of his whispering her name sent her lonely body into overdrive? Dawn Summers wasn't there for his amusement.

This time she wouldn't get her judgment clouded by girlish fantasies. Richard was a job to her and nothing else. If he thought for one moment something else might happen, he was out of his mind. The faster he figured it out, the better off his sexy ass would be. *Damn, I need to stop thinking about how gorgeous he is or I won't get one thing done,* her mind thought as the ringing doorbell intruded on her private fantasy.

* * * *

The breeze dried some of the sweat from his body, but the majority of it was still damp as he ran down the well-lit street. Richard loved his nightly run; it gave his mind the peace it needed to sort through the events of the day. The most important thought in his mind now was a way to get Dawn interested in him. Today, she had let him kiss her, but she didn't kiss him back. That wasn't a good sign at all. Dawn acted like she felt nothing towards him. Had he really killed what she used to feel for him?

He couldn't work in close quarters with her and not be attracted. Brad was right. All his criticism of her was his way of trying to fight the attraction he felt for her in the past.

But now, Dawn seemed hell bent on keeping their relationship on the business level. Furthermore, who had she gone out on a date with yesterday? He didn't like competing with a guy he knew nothing about. How long had they been seeing each other? Was it serious enough that he was about to buy her a ring? All the questions needed to be answered, and he would get the answers he wanted from Dawn at work tomorrow.

Richard stopped and did a few stretches for his cramped muscles. He couldn't stop his mind from wandering back to the kiss he shared with Dawn. His mouth still tingled from how passionate it was on his part. If he had a few more minutes, Dawn would have felt the same way. He knew she still remembered the nasty words he yelled at her. Thinking back, he knew that Melissa and Emily had been the problem when it came to Dawn. In all honestly, Dawn was doing her job when she pulled Melissa to the side to discuss her problems at *D4*.

Melissa, being the bitch she was, had torn into Dawn, making her doubt her abilities as a manager. He couldn't let the situation stay the way Dawn left it back at the restaurant. If they didn't settle it, they would never be able to work together. *D4* had a long way to go to get back to the level it was when Dawn was manager.

Standing under the streetlight, he looked up and down the street for any signs of the woman haunting his mind. He knew Dawn lived on the next street. He was hoping that if he made a surprise appearance she might be in the mood to talk to him.

Jogging over one block, Richard paused at the corner. His eyes got hard at the sight in front of Dawn's house. She was standing there, hugging some man by a parked car. He didn't seem to be much older than she. Separating their bodies, the guy leaned down to kiss Dawn on her cheek and then moved back. The stranger waited until she got safely into the house before driving off. Seeing red, Richard ran to Dawn's house and knocked loudly on the door.

* * * *

"Hey, did you forget something?" Dawn laughed as she opened the door to a gorgeous, sweaty, and very pissed off Richard Drace.

"Who in the hell was that guy?" he asked, coming into her house and slamming the door behind him.

Folding her arms, Dawn stared at him. "Do you know how late it is? Why are you at my house at seven-thirty at night? Did you need to ask me something about *D4*?"

Dawn hoped she would be able to hear Richard's answer over the pounding of her heart. He looked so stirring with the sweat clinging to his damp T-shirt. Sweaty men never used to get her blood racing, but the towering man trying to control his temper in front of her changed that. Thoughts of peeling the shirt from his body would keep her dreaming for hours tonight, but she wasn't about to let him see it in her face or eyes.

"Don't answer my question with a question," he growled, advancing towards her, but Dawn stood her ground.

"Is that what I did?" she asked, her smile showing a dimple in her left cheek.

Reaching out, Richard tugged her to him. "You know what you're doing," he muttered softly.

"Richard, are you sure I know what I'm doing?" she asked, throwing in another dimpled grin.

Brushing his lips very lightly over her, he sipped the essence from her body into his. "Did he kiss you?" he asked hotly.

Twisting her head away from him and shoving at Richard's hard chest, Dawn ended the embrace. "You have no right to show up at my house this late at night and inquire about my personal life. What I do outside the restaurant is my own business. I don't have to answer to you," she finished with a finger poke to his chest. "Now, if you have a question about D4, I can answer that, but anything else falls under 'none of your damn business.'"

"Are you going to tell me who he is?" he asked for the final time.

She gazed back at him without blinking. "I guess I can take that as a no," he said, going back toward the front door. Richard opened the door and stood there a few moments; he allowed the cool air to calm down his heated body. "I have to find a way to tame that temper of yours," he threw back over his shoulder.

Dawn rushed to the door to give him a small shove, helping him all the way outside. "I'm not an animal. Don't you dare say I need to be tamed," she yelled at his back.

Richard walked until he got to the end of her pathway. Turning back around, he looked at her. "Dawn, you're like a hurt kitten now, but with a few strokes in the right places, I'll have you purring in my hands. And don't doubt that I can do it," he said with a hint of seduction in his irresistible drawl. He strolled away without looking back, because he could feel Dawn's eyes on his back all the way to the corner.

Slamming the door hard, Dawn hated Richard because she believed him. Just saying those few words had made her want to yank him back in there and rip the clothes from his body.

"Girl, you have to fight those urges that man sends to your body. Remember, Richard is only doing it because he needs your help with D4. Once he has his restaurant back up and running, he won't ever look at you twice."

Tapping two fingers against her temple, she whispered, "Stay focused. Please let tomorrow come slowly. I can't take Richard in this flirtatious mood." Feeling stressed, she decided to take a nice milk bath. Those always helped calm her nerves after a long, hard, stressful day, and Richard's surprise appearance just turned her night into one.

"Richard, you aren't going to win. I have more willpower than you think," Dawn said. But who was she trying to convince? Richard or herself?

Chapter Four

"Damn, where is some help when you need it?" Richard growled early the next morning as he glared at the closed office door. He was trying to juggle his morning paper, hot, black coffee, and a bag of donuts while struggling to push open the door. Finally, on the third attempt, the door flew open, almost causing him to drop the coffee on the floor. He was glad it didn't happen, because he wasn't the nicest guy until after his first cup of caffeine in the morning.

Walking into the office, he was stunned to see Dawn there, sitting at his desk, already writing notes down in the pad of hers. "Did you not hear me fighting with the door?" he asked.

Looking up, she replied, "I didn't think the trainer wanted nor needed help from the person he thought needed taming."

"Baby, that mouth of yours is going to get you in trouble," he warned.

"It hasn't yet," she replied, winking at him.

If you knew what I was thinking, you wouldn't be winking at me, he thought. Tossing the donuts down on the table, Richard took a sip of his coffee. "Why are you dressed like that?" he questioned, taking in her pulled-back hair, unflattering shirt, and horrible, colorless skirt. "You look like some spinster from a romance novel," he teased.

Pushing up the glasses, she gave him a cold look. "I thought if I looked more the part of a restaurant manager, you might take me more seriously instead of always touching or kissing me."

Standing back, Richard tossed the empty coffee container across the room, landing it perfectly into the trashcan without touching the rim.

Laughing, he stalked over to Dawn. "Kitten, I could care less about what clothes you place on your body. What I'm always thinking about now, since you came back, is how to get you out of them," he admitted, opening a button on her stiff shirt.

Her eyes widened behind the glasses. "You're lying," she whispered.

Bringing his eyes up to hers, he said, "Yes, you're right; I am lying," he admitted, working another button loose while he had Dawn's attention.

"See, I knew you weren't to be trusted," she snapped, getting up from the desk. Dawn tried to brush past him.

Pressing his body to hers, he backed her up to the desk. "At least let me finish before you storm off," he suggested. *Come on, Kitten, let me stroke you.*

Dawn's eyes narrowed at him, daring him to piss her off even more. "Truthfully, I have wanted you since the first day you started working for me, but I didn't want to admit it." He leaned down to nibble at the part of her neck not covered by the shirt.

Closing her eyes, Dawn allowed herself to enjoy this time in Richard's arms. It might not ever happen again. "Stop playing with me," she moaned.

"Dump that guy from last night, and let me show you how it feels to be with a man, not a boy," he whispered, thrusting his lower body to hers. "I promise I'll be better than any dream you've had in the past," he stated, pulling her earlobe into his moist, hot mouth.

"No," she muttered, shoving at his chest. "I can't do this." Fixing her shirt, Dawn put some distance between their bodies. "Richard, I meant what I said yesterday. If we can't work together without you coming on to me, then I need to leave. I want this job, but I don't want you," she said to his face.

Hurt that Dawn wasn't responding to his advances, Richard hit her the only way that he knew he could—with his words. His voice was cold when he spat, "Don't worry. I won't make another move for you again, Miss Summers. Emily is more than enough woman for me to handle. I was only trying to give you a little incentive by kissing you," he lied.

"A woman like you could never get a man like me, and I hope you know that," Richard snickered as he sat down at his desk. He tried not to see the hurt that appeared in Dawn's eyes.

Pain clouded Dawn's eyes, but her voice was strong. "Yes, I think I remember you saying something like that to me before. Let me go and grab some folders from my car, and we can get started," she told him, going out the door and closing it softly behind her.

"Shit! Why you can't keep your mouth shut?" Richard asked himself. He saw Dawn's face close up at his harsh words, but it was too late to take them back. They were already there, hanging above both their heads. Her perfume was still lingering by his desk, driving him crazy, and her skin was so soft each time he got the chance to touch it. Whatever she used on it was made to drive a man crazy.

Over the years, the Drace brothers had earned labels from the people of Houston. Lee was the overbearing older brother. Zack was the laid-back one until he was pushed, but now he was happily married to his beautiful wife Traci, with a baby on the way. Brad, the baby, was the carefree one, because he never took anything too seriously and lived each day to the fullest.

Then there was him: the nice one, always there to help his brothers no matter the problem. However, Dawn wouldn't say he was nice to her. A flash of loneliness stabbed at him. He wasn't the guy he had shown to Dawn. Yet, it was too late to start over with her, and she probably wouldn't let him anyway. So he would get through working with her and send her on with a good reference. Dawn didn't need him.

"I found what I was looking for," Dawn said, coming back into the office. "Let's sit at the table so we can get started."

As he came around the desk, Richard noticed she had taken her hair down and undone two buttons on the horrible white shirt; it made her look so much better. Pulling out a chair, he waited for her to sit before taking a seat beside her.

"Thank you," Dawn told him as she sat down. He nodded at her but didn't answer. "I think we need to start from the beginning to find a way to better to market D4. We both know it can make money because you always had a packed place when I worked here.

"What we need to do is find that missing ingredient again. Now, I think the business went down some due to the fact the word of mouth stopped after it opened," she pointed out, looking at sales statements from around the third month of business.

"Also, you had way too many employees trying to do the same job at the same time, and it became confusing," Dawn pointed out, showing him some numbers on her notepad. "I don't think I can go back through and fix the mistakes, so it would be best to try a new way."

Richard looked at the woman to whom he really hadn't spoken a kind word since their first meeting, working hard to help him out. He sucked his breath in deeply as he smelled the scent of raspberries coming off Dawn and knew he truly didn't want her to leave after she helped him. He wanted her to stay with him for as long as she would have him.

"Dawn, I'm sorry for the way I've treated you," Richard apologized, glancing over at her. He didn't say those words often, and they felt foreign to his tongue. "I shouldn't have kissed you like I did yesterday. It wasn't professional and I know now you didn't want it."

Dawn stopped writing with the pen in midair because Richard's apology came out of left field. He didn't apologize for his actions. Not once while she had worked for him in the past had she heard him utter those words. "Thank you, Richard," she commented.

A smile briefly touched his firm lips, then it went away just as fast. "Can you tell me what you have come up with so far?" he asked, pointing to the pad in front of her. He leaned closer to the pad to get a better look at Dawn's handwriting. A new pair of glasses was in his desk, but he couldn't bring himself to wear them in front of Dawn. It wouldn't give him the appearance he wanted around her.

They made him look older than his thirty-two years, and he didn't like to look any older than he was. There was already an age gap between them that he didn't care much for. It wasn't a huge difference, but it still bothered him.

"Why aren't you wearing those glasses I saw in your desk?" Dawn asked, peeping at him from the corner of her eye.

Frowning, Richard wondered how to answer her question without sounding too arrogant. It wasn't something he wanted to do yet in his life, because he felt he was too young to need reading glasses. "I really don't need them. I don't know why my doctor prescribed them in the first place," he complained.

"Well, I thought they would make you look very handsome," she commented, tapping her pen on the notepad as though hoping he would take the hint.

Richard couldn't believe Dawn was trying to trick him into placing those ugly things on his face. "I'm not placing those horrible things on my face because I know I won't look attractive," he said with a hint of sarcasm.

Blinking, Dawn stared him from behind hers. "Are you saying I'm not pretty when I wear mine to read?" she teased lightly.

Squirming around in his chair, Richard looked everywhere but her face. Dawn had to know that her glasses made her look so cute and adorable. They enhanced the color of her eyes even more. "You know that you look very pretty with or without them," he said with a little heat to his voice.

"Good. I feel the same about you," she said. "Now go get those glasses so you don't have to strain your eyes to see the paper." Dawn gave him a little shove, causing him to get up from the chair.

After taking the glasses out of the desk and shoving them on his face, Richard had to admit that when he sat back down, the writing on the pad did look much clearer than it had the first time.

Hiding her smile, Dawn started to point out the things she wanted to go over with him. "Do you want to take notes?" she asked him.

"No, I'll just make a copy of your information if that's okay with you," Richard replied.

Shrugging her shoulders, Dawn laid out her plans. D4 could be saved, but a lot of work had to be done to make it work. "What I'm wondering is, did you ask yourself enough tough and important questions before you decided to start D4? A lot of heavy planning goes into starting any business. But, owning a restaurant is one of the hardest jobs a person can have, and I want to be positive that you want this as much as I think you do," Dawn said, turning to face him.

"Yes, I want to help you in any way I can to save my restaurant," Richard stressed. He tried his best to stay calm because it felt odd taking advice from a woman. Even though he knew Dawn was first-rate at her job, something about it still didn't sit well with him. However, his pride could be pushed to the back to save his place of business.

"Lay it all out for me so I can see what I have to do," Richard stated, sliding his seat beside hers. "Think of my mind as a lump of clay that you can mold into the perfect restaurant owner," he teased with a wink.

"Are you sure?" Dawn asked, pausing to give him enough time to back out.

"Positive," he answered. "I wanted you back for a reason. No matter what occurred between us in the past, I know you're the best person for the managerial job at *D4*, and that's the reason I wanted you back so badly. Don't worry about me calling rank on you again. I made that mistake one time, and look where it landed me. There aren't enough customers coming in anymore to even keep the doors open seven days a week. Any of your suggestions I'm going to be willing to try, because you know how to run my business better than I did. Why would I say no to one word that comes out of that pretty mouth of yours?" he flirted. He tried not to tease Dawn, but he couldn't help it, not when she was sitting so close looking this good.

"Richard," Dawn's voice warned.

"Sorry," Richard apologized, holding up his hands. "It's a bad habit I have," he told her. "I love flirting with an attractive woman. Dawn, you have to know that I find you extremely good-looking, but I know you aren't here for that." He cut off her response. "I'll try to keep it at a business level as much as I can," he said with a weak promise by her ear.

Chapter Five

Choosing to ignore Richard's tempting voice, Dawn continued on with her advice. "At least you're doing the first step in good business correctly," she said. "You're willing to take the advice I want to give with an open mind and not think that you know it all. Most people who won't take good recommendations are doomed to fail from the beginning." Pulling out a sheet of paper from a blue folder, she placed it between their bodies. Richard's cologne was slowly driving her crazy, but she was keeping her head about herself.

Once she got home tonight, she could fantasize about Richard all she wanted. However, this was the workplace, and work would be done. Relaxing her tense body again, Dawn used her pen to point out a few things to him.

"I noticed that your brother Lee invested some money into the restaurant, and I think that's wonderful, but what about asking another brother and maybe a friend? I think having outside investors help with making better decisions. They are able to see more than one viewpoint. Also, maybe they know more facts about the restaurant business than either one of us do." Stopping, Dawn watched

Richard's face for any kind of reaction about what she had said so far. "Do you have any questions?"

* * * *

Richard didn't want to ask anyone else for money. It made him seem like a failure at his business. Why couldn't this just stay between the two of them? Lee really didn't have to know why *D4* was having problems, either. Richard knew that he had enough money in the bank to give Lee's startup money back if he had to. "Can't the problem stay in this room?" he questioned.

"We need outside help if you want to get this place back up and running in under a year. I won't lie and say we don't," Dawn told him honestly.

"Are you saying I'm a failure?" Richard asked hotly.

"You aren't a failure," she said, touching his hand on top of the table. "It takes a strong person to ask for help."

Proud eyes gazed back at him, and he looked for any sign of lies, but he only saw warmth reflected back at him. Sighing, he placed his hand on top of hers, lightly running a finger across the back. "How many more people would I need?" he asked through clenched teeth.

"Well, I think two should be enough to help you," she advised him, removing her hand and placing it in her lap. "Another task that needs to be done is to go back and rethink the structure of *D4*."

Richard didn't understand what Dawn was taking about; he liked how his restaurant looked in general. The location was perfect for the number of customers he wanted to draw on a nightly basis. He never wanted a huge establishment, but more of a cozy feel, where families or business meetings could be accommodated at a moment's notice.

It was sounding like Dawn wanted him to change the entire setup of his place, and that wouldn't happen. "I don't like where you're going with this," he said. "*D4*'s structure is fine the way it is."

* * * *

Dawn heard the unyielding tone of Richard's voice. She had thought about this long and hard before she decided to bring this up. Hopefully, after he heard her plans, it would change his mind, too. "Richard, I think you might need to make *D4* a little bit bigger to accommodate more events or organizations. The bigger it is, the more business it will draw in for you."

He opened his mouth to argue, but Dawn held up her hand to stop him. "Don't misunderstand what I'm telling you," she rushed out. "Your restaurant can still have the cozy atmosphere that you want, but also provide another option for the bigger clients or people who may want to rent it on certain nights. Having more than one service will draw more people to spend money here, and the more money spent is the more money for you to have in your accounts."

Sliding a typed document across the table, Dawn let him read how much more money *D4* could bring in if they tried her plan. Reading over the statement and figures, Richard raised shocked eyes to hers. "Are you sure I'll be able to draw this kind of money in?" he asked, astonished.

"Yes. I did some research on the Internet, and you're in the best spot to draw in huge amounts, along with keeping the values you wanted for the business."

* * * *

Grinning, Dawn took her glasses off, tossing them on the stack of papers in front of her. Richard was taken aback by the beauty of her chocolate-brown skin. She had to be the most beautiful woman he had ever seen, but she wasn't even interested in dating him now.

It was all back business between the two of them. He knew that in the past seeing him had placed the same look of pleasure of her face, yet now she only saw him as a paycheck and future reference. *I have to get you back in my life. You aren't meant to leave me a second time. Zack went after the woman he wanted, and hell, I'm going to do the same thing.*

Richard gave her a smile, and Dawn returned it, oblivious to what was going on in his mind. "When do you want to get all this rolling?" he asked, looking at the paper one last time before placing it on the table.

"Well, let me do a little more research, and I think I can have more information for you by the end of the week."

A thought passed in his mind. "Did you know that the building next door is empty and was up for sale? I think Zack brought it the middle of last year and doesn't know what to do with it. What if I see about buying it from him and we can connect *D4* to it?" Richard suggested.

Getting caught up in the excitement, she hugged Richard. "I think that's a wonderful idea."

Wrapping his arms around her, he pulled her tempting body to his, loving the feel of her in his arms. Dawn felt so right against him that he never wanted to let her go. Sliding his fingers through her thick, black hair, he breathed in her scent, placing a light kiss on her neck because he couldn't resist the urge to taste her.

She stiffened instantly. "I don't think you should do that," Dawn said, moving away from him.

* * * *

"I got caught up in the moment." Richard grinned, showing off his amazing eyes.

Dawn tried her best not to feel anything when she was near him, but it was hard to deny the attraction. "Trying to refrain from doing it again, okay?" she suggested in a stern voice. Turning her head, Dawn started gathering up all the paperwork. They had worked steadily for hours, and now it was lunchtime.

She would be late for her appointment. "I need to leave, and I'll see you back here at one o'clock," Dawn said, grabbing her purse off the back of the chair as she got up and went to the door.

"Do you want to have lunch with me?" Richard inquired, standing up to stop her from leaving.

Twirling back around, Dawn stared at the man who still had a piece of her heart, "Sorry, I can't. I already have a date," she said, rushing out the door.

* * * *

"What's wrong with you?" Zack asked his brother, who wouldn't have summoned him to *D4* for lunch unless it was for something important. He had to cancel a lunch date with his gorgeous, pregnant wife to come over here. Luckily, Traci had other plans and didn't mind that he cancelled at the last second.

"I know you love the hamburger and fries from that diner by my office. Since you're not eating, I guess you're having problems. Is it Emily?" Zack asked, taking a bite of his club sandwich.

"No, I'm having problems with Dawn," Richard snapped.

Swallowing his food, Zack raised an eyebrow. "So, Brad wasn't lying at dinner last night. He did walk in on you and Dawn pressed together." He laughed.

Richard's eyes narrowed dangerously. "You have never met Dawn, so don't say another word about her."

The smile vanished from his brother's face. "You're in love with her, aren't you?"

Without missing a beat, Richard said, "Yes, I think I am, and now she doesn't want anything to do with me. Hell, I even think she's dating someone," his deep voice rumbled.

"Well, she didn't leave here on the best of terms, if I recall correctly. You had a lot of harsh words to say to her," Zack pointed out, taking another bite of his food.

Richard looked at his brother. "I thought that Traci was the one who was pregnant, not you."

"Very funny, little brother," Zack said, tossing the empty plate into the trash. "I have started to eat more since she got pregnant," he admitted. "I've always been so connected to her, so maybe that's why I feel everything she does and crave more food now, too."

"Do you know what you're having?" Richard couldn't wait until his niece or nephew was born.

"No, we go back in a couple of weeks to find out," Zack said with a huge smile. "I don't care either way as long as the baby is healthy. But if I have a choice, I would love to have a son."

Richard felt a little jealous of his brother. Zack had found the love of his life, but his soul mate was fighting him and dating someone else on the side. *Damn it!* He would find a way to end whatever the two of them had going on, and the sooner the better. "I know you didn't invite me to lunch to discuss Traci's pregnancy, so why am I here, Richard?"

"Have you sold the building next door yet?"

Zack could see the light shining behind Richard's eyes, "No, I haven't, and truthfully, I was starting to regret getting the space anyway."

Leaning across the desk, Richard couldn't keep the hope out of his voice. "Do you think you could let me buy it from you? Dawn's thinking about expanding *D4*, and the extra room would be a bonus for us."

"Sorry, I can't sell it to you," Zack said with a straight face.

"Why not?" Richard muttered, falling back into his chair. He knew Zack always had doubts about him as a businessman, but his saying no that quickly came as a total shock.

"I want you to take it as part of my investment in *D4*, along with this check," he said, pulling it out of his jacket. "I had read about *D4* in the papers and was upset you hadn't come to me for help. We're brothers, and we need to look out for each other," Zack said, tossing the huge check down on the desk. "I've done well over the past few years. What's wrong with me wanting to help out my brother? And I owe you."

Richard didn't understand Zack's words. "Why do you owe me?"

"That night at the gym; if you hadn't made me go after Traci and ask her out, I wouldn't be married to the most extraordinary woman in the world," Zack stated.

He had forgotten all about that night at the gym. It was such a long time ago. Richard picked up Zack's check. "I'll pay you back every penny after we get *D4* back up and running," he promised him, shoving the check inside the desk.

Zack stood up. "I better go and check on Traci. I think she's having lunch with her sister."

Richard laughed because Cherise was totally different from her sweet-natured sister. "Cherise's personality has changed a little since she first meet you," he pointed out, walking his brother through the place and out the front door.

"Yeah, she's a little more accepting of me now and really is happy about the baby, but she and Lee still can't be in the same room without fighting," Zack replied.

"Do you think they are ever going to realize what's going on between them?" Richard questioned Zack by his car.

"Lee knows he's attracted to Cherise, but I don't know if he thinks it's love," Zack laughed. Lee would be the last of them to admit that he was in love with their sister-in-law.

"I can't wait until it hits him between the eyes, because once it does, he'll do anything to win her over," Richard admitted, thinking of his own problems with Dawn.

Zack laid his hand on his brother's shoulder as a car drove into the parking lot. "Don't give up. I know you'll win her over." He noticed an attractive woman getting out, and watched how Richard's eyes never left her as she moved towards them.

As she hurried past them, she muttered, "Sorry, I'm late."

"Wait a minute, Dawn. I want you to meet my brother," Richard yelled, waving her over to him.

Dawn's shoulders hunched over when Richard yelled for her. It was as though she didn't want to be introduced to him, but she came over anyway.

"Dawn Summers, I would like for you to meet my older brother, Zack Drace," Richard said proudly. "Zack, meet my brilliant manager, Dawn Summers."

Dawn looked at Zack quickly, visibly taken back by his brother's compliment before shaking his hand. "Nice to meet you, Zack," she smiled. "I think I may have seen you at D4 a few times, but I don't think I ever knew who you were."

"Yes, you were in Richard's office, I believe," Zack replied, ending the handshake.

"Well, it was nice to meet you," Dawn said. Turning to Richard, she said, "I'll see you back inside when you're finished talking to your brother." Dawn left them standing there and went through the front door without looking back.

"Wow, she's gorgeous up close. Are you sure she'll want a loser like you?" Zack joked, shoving his brother in the shoulder.

"Hey, if someone as ugly as you can get Traci, I know I can't miss with Dawn. You know that I've always been the best-looking brother in the family," Richard said, teasing him back.

Zack laughed at his brother's humor. "Dawn seems nice, so why did you always complain about her?" Zack asked, leaning on his car hood.

"Back then, I was listening to several people instead of my mind, and now it may be too late to fix things. Every day around lunchtime, she leaves for a date, and it kills me not knowing who it's with," he admitted, glancing back at the restaurant. Richard hated how he had let others control his mind all those months ago, and now, when he was ready to pursue a relationship with Dawn, she wasn't interested.

"I have a question for you," Richard said.

"What is it?" Zack asked, folding his arms across his chest.

"Do you think I should just give up on Dawn?"

"No, I would give it all I had and go after her with everything I had in me."

"Dawn only wants us to be business associates, and if I can't do that, then she'll leave without helping me save *D4*. Also, she doesn't want me to flirt with her while we're working." Richard groaned under his breath. "That isn't going to work."

Laughing, Zack unlocked his car door and then slid behind the wheel and closed the door. "You have her on the run, man, and you don't even know it," he informed his baby brother. "Dawn's telling you not to touch her because she's still attracted to you."

A relieved smile spread across Richard's face. "Are you positive about this?"

Zack nodded. "Yes, I'm sure, but let on that you know it, and she'll fight you even more. Just play it down like she wants you to, but every once in a while, kiss or touch her when she's not expecting you to. The suspense of when it will happen next will drive her crazy," he said, starting his car.

Richard moved out of the way so his brother could pull out of the parking lot. Standing there, he watched his brother drive off, and it made him think about the struggle Zack went through to win Traci over. Maybe his advice wasn't all wrong, but not touching Dawn when her smooth skin called for his fingers would be hard. There was something about her that begged for tenderness from him, yet she pushed him away at every turn.

What was going on with her? Why did she leave every afternoon for lunch and come back ten minutes late? Was she out with the guy he saw at her house? God, what if they were making love? No, she wouldn't do that to him. Storming back to the front door, he flung it open and rushed back to his office because he needed to talk to Dawn, and it couldn't wait.

* * * *

"Listen, I can't meet with you now," Dawn yelled into her cell phone.

"I need you to come back," the person said.

"I just left from having lunch with you and was late coming back to work. My boss isn't going to allow me to keep coming back late like this."

"Dawn, I really need to talk to you. You shouldn't have left so early."

"Yes, I know you want to talk to me, but I can't right now." Running her fingers through her hair, Dawn walked over to the window, still on the phone.

"Either come back or else." The threat came across loud and clear.

"Don't you dare threaten me," she hissed.

"It's your fault, and why won't you admit it?"

"No, it isn't my fault." Calming down, she spoke in a softer voice. "Think about what you're saying, and you'll see how crazy it sounds. You can't actually think I'll do that now," she said, shocked.

"I'm not crazy. You were the one who wanted to do this and not me."

"I know I was the one who came to you, but things are different now," she admitted.

"Either come to me, or I'll come there and have a talk with Richard. I know you wouldn't want that."

Closing her eyes, Dawn massaged her temples with her free hand. "Fine, I'll see you at my house around six o'clock," she snapped, ending the call. Spinning around, she found Richard standing behind her.

"Who was that on the phone?" he asked, easing further into his office.

She clamped her jaw tight and stared at the man she didn't want to see at the moment. "Let's not get involved with each other's personal business, okay?

I'm here to help with *D4*, not discuss my private phone conversation," she snapped, shoving the phone into her purse.

Richard's firm mouth took on an unpleasant twist at her words. "I was only trying to show interest in my employee. Don't worry, it won't happen again, Miss Summers," he retorted, retaking his seat back at the table.

Dawn held back tears of frustration at the mess she had made of her life; the man she was in love with was slowly beginning to hate her, and the other problems she was having couldn't be ignored much longer.

"I noticed you didn't get a chance to eat your lunch," she said, pointing at the untouched hamburger on his desk.

"I thought we were going to deal with business and not anything personal," he countered.

Dawn chose her words carefully. "Richard, I was wrong to yell at you," she apologized, sitting down. "I should have left what happened at my lunch date there, and I didn't. It won't happen again," she informed him, tossing her pad down on the table.

Closing off any expressions, she brought their conversation back to *D4*. "Did you get a chance to ask Zack about the property next door?" She had to keep her mind on helping Richard and not that phone call. She could deal with that after she got home.

Richard regarded Dawn quizzically for a moment. "I can't sit here and not ask about how your lunch went," Richard said. Dawn gave him a warning look, but he still continued. "I came into my office and you were yelling into the phone. Don't say a word until I finish," he warned, looking at her. "I can't work with you and not care about you. I heard when you said we can't be more than employer and employee, and much as it hurts me, I'll do as you requested. However, I hope we can slowly work towards a friendship," he insisted. "Can you become my friend while you're working here? Please? I won't ask for anything more from you. I promise." He stood, then pulled her into his arms, holding her close.

Dawn turned her head away, wearied by indecision. Richard didn't know what was going on with her now and to pull him into the middle of it would be wrong. Yet, the strong comfort of his arms felt so good. He was really the only person she truly knew in Houston. Would it be so bad to allow him in her life for a little while?

"What would this friendship involve?" she asked, looking back at him.

Richard's eyes closed slowly as he breathed the words "thank you" into Dawn's sweet-smelling hair. "We'll talk to each other when the other person is having problems. Maybe a lunch or two, with a dinner thrown in for fun," he answered, brushing her thick hair back from her cheek.

Shaking her head, Dawn said, "I'm not too sure about the dinners while we're working together. It may not be the best idea, Richard."

His voice was carefully calm when he answered her. "Dawn, business associates have dinner together all the time," he reassured her.

Biting her lip, she looked away, uncertain. "Are you sure the dinner will just be about business and nothing else?" Dawn questioned, still a little apprehensive about saying yes to him. Richard had a way of making her say yes when the word *no* should be coming out of her mouth instead. He did have a hidden charm about him that he knew how to use to win her over each and every time.

"No, I can't promise you that," he answered honestly. "I might get the urge to kiss those sexy lips of yours." He moaned as he lightly brushed his firm ones against her softer ones.

Pushing him back from her, Dawn was uncomfortable with the fact that he'd spoken the truth and that she wanted to hear those words. "I have to think about the dinner dates, but I don't see anything against us having lunch."

Richard grinned at her. "Good, I thought you might put up more of a battle, and I'm glad you didn't. Let's move on to business," he said. "I talked to Zack, and he's going to let us have the building as an investment, along with a check that I stuck in my desk." He went over to his desk and opened the top drawer.

She only half-listened as she struggled with her conscience about saying yes to Richard so fast. Shouldn't she have made him ask more than once? She always gave in to him so easily. "Can you find a contractor to connect the two places for the price of the check?" he questioned, coming back and writing the amount down on her pad.

Drawing her attention back to the conversation, she looked at the amount. "Are you sure this amount is correct?" she choked out.

"Yes, I asked the same thing when I saw it," Richard admitted. "Zack said he wanted to make a big investment in *D4*."

"I think this should be enough to do all the work I wanted, along with having a little left over for extra items I didn't think we'll be able to do." She grinned. Dawn always loved the restaurant business, and to be able to work with this amount of cash made all her dreams come true. Hopefully, Richard would be pleased with the finished results.

"There are still several things we have to go over on this list before we can call it a day," she said, tapping a pen on the pad.

Richard went back over to his work area and retook his seat. "I don't have anyone I need to rush home to. Do you?" he asked.

Dawn peeked at him from across the room. "I have to leave by six o'clock. Someone is expecting me for dinner."

"Would it be that guy I saw you with at your house?" Richard asked, sounding jealous.

"Please, can we not get into this?"

"Dawn, you just make sure this guy knows that you're mine until I say you aren't, and I don't have a problem at all with your dinner guest."

Her pulse began to beat erratically at the threatening promise in Richard's deep voice. She had never heard him use that tone before. "Umm...you don't have any say in whom I go out with," Dawn said, hoping to calm him down a little.

Leaning forward, Richard trapped her with the look in his eyes. "I'll let you believe that for a little while longer. But then I'll show you whom you really belong to," he murmured quietly, startling her.

Moving back, Richard picked up his pen and started writing down plans he wanted to use the extra money for. Dawn couldn't allow Richard to plan their future when there wasn't going to be one, not if she didn't deal with her current problem.

Standing up, she went around the side of the desk so she could talk to Richard and make him understand. She laid her hand on him; the muscles of his forearm hardened beneath the sleeve.

"Baby, do you know what your touch does to my body?" he hissed.

"No, why don't you tell us what her touch does," Emily said, coming into the room, breaking the magic of the moment. She slid her purse from her shoulder, tossing it into the chair.

Dawn dropped her hand, turning to look at the younger woman. Emily was a perfect contrast to Richard's dark looks. Her strawberry blonde hair had a windblown look, and her outfit showed everything she had to offer.

"I think I should leave," Dawn said, stepping away from Richard. Her mind and body weren't up to dealing with Emily today.

Richard's hand shot out to grab her wrist. "You don't have to leave," he said, under his breath, his eyes pleading with her to stay with him.

"Your girlfriend is here now, and it's four-thirty, so it's time for me to leave," Dawn said.

Seconds stretched by until Richard finally let go of Dawn's wrist. "I'll see you tomorrow," he told her as she inched away from him and gathered up her belongings. Dawn didn't answer him as she went out the door past Emily, who looked at her and laughed.

* * * *

"Why do you tease her like that?" Emily giggled, coming across the room and kissing him on the cheek.

"To what do I owe this pleasure of this visit?" he asked, throwing his cold lunch into the trash.

"I wanted to invite you to dinner," Emily said, sliding on the end of his desk, showing off long, tanned legs in a short white skirt. There was a time her legs would have driven him crazy, but he never had the urge to do anything more than look at her. Dawn was the one he wanted naked in his bed.

"I can't have dinner with you," he said, picking up his appointment book. Richard eased past Emily's body, trying to think of a way to get rid of her.

"Why can't you?" Emily asked, pouting. "I was going to fix your favorite meal. I have everything waiting back at my place," she said, brushing the front of her body against the back of his.

Richard stiffened at her touch and scent. Emily advertised what she had to offer way too much for his taste. He loved the way Dawn was so sexy without showing off her body to the point of being a slut. "You know how much I hate it when you do that," he snapped, moving away.

Emily blinked hard at Richard's harshness with her. "Are you upset Dawn didn't want to stay here with you?" Emily asked, narrowing her sea-foam green eyes. "You aren't serious about her, are you? She has nothing to offer you but drama. That's all those women know about," she snickered with a roll of her eyes.

Pausing at the door, Richard said in a low voice, "Emily, if you want to still be considered a welcome customer at *D4* when it reopens, then you won't say another nasty word about Dawn." Richard continued out the door, waiting for Emily to follow so he could lock up the place.

"I'm going to be more than a customer, Richard. I'll be your wife by the time *D4* reopens, and that's a promise."

Chapter Six

Shutting the door after her dinner guest had left, Dawn stood there amazed and shaken. It wasn't going to be as easy as she thought, getting herself out of this problem. Why in the hell did she fall for Richard Drace in the first damn place? It was his fault that she was in the situation, and he didn't even know it. God, why did she do it? Sure, he had said a few harsh words to her, but nothing he had ever said was bad as this.

For the past several years, she had been so proud of herself for no longer making rash judgments, but sticking with her goals. However, that one day at *D4* had changed her life. "What am I going to do?" she asked herself.

Closing her eyes, Dawn rested her head on the front door, trying to think of a way out of this problem. How many times in her twenty-nine years had her mother told her not to make rash decisions? Too many for her to count, even using both hands. Making quick choices was a part of her past until Richard Drace strolled into her life…or did she barrel into his? It was so hard to determine which one really happened.

All that she knew was this mistake had to be fixed quickly, or it would haunt her for the rest of her life. Pushing herself away from the door, Dawn took a seat, and her eyes scanned over the notes she wanted to discuss with Richard first thing in the morning. So far he had agreed to every suggestion she tossed his way, which really surprised her. He loved having his way about *D4*, but something had happened to make him more agreeable with her.

In the past, he always had such a strong opinion about the way things needed to be done; furthermore, he disliked change unless he thought it would benefit *D4* in a positive way. She understood he would be apprehensive about changes in his business because the restaurant was his baby and he loved it very much. Yet, on the plus side, Richard was very willing to work long hard hours and to fulfill duties on any ideas she had about *D4*.

Tomorrow she would ask him if he talked to the contractor about connecting the two buildings. It might take the whole check his brother Zack gave him as an investment. The quality she loved the most about him was how dependable he was with following through on tasks. Back when she had worked for him, he had always done assignments almost to perfection when she had suggestions about meals or how seating should be arranged to make the place look better.

But when it came to helping her deal with the difficult employees, he turned on her, which still amazed her. It was in the past, and she would leave it there. *D4* needed to be saved, and that what she was going to do. All her other problems would just take a back seat until she thought of a way to get out of them. Hopefully by next week, she would get the good news she wanted to hear.

* * * *

"Brad told me about how he found you and Dawn in your office," Lee told Richard over dinner that night. They were the only two there because Zack and Traci were having dinner with her sister to celebrate her new job.

Brad was out on a date with a secretary from the workplace. Richard thought he could come to Lee's house and not hear Dawn's name, yet it didn't happen. "Brad needs to keep his mouth shut," Richard snapped, shoving the pasta into his mouth. Chewing, he gave Lee a hard look, daring him to say another word. However, Lee wasn't scared, especially since he was taller by three inches.

"Hey, I'm not saying anything is wrong with her," Lee exclaimed. "I think the one time I came to the restaurant to talk to you, I saw her outside having a heated conversation with some guy."

Richard dropped his fork down on the table. "Do you remember what the guy looked like?" he asked, thinking it might be the same guy he saw at her house.

"No, it was dark, and his back was to me," Lee informed him. "I only saw Dawn's face because she was facing the parking lot. What's with all the questions?" Lee asked, taking a sip of his drink. "Has Dawn already done something, or are you trying to figure out the competition?"

Richard didn't answer Lee. Instead, he took another bite of his pasta. Lee had had the same cook for the past three years, and the man knew how to fix a pasta dinner. He loved going over on Wednesday nights because of this mouth-watering meal.

"No, I'm not wondering about the competition," Richard answered, shoving his empty plate away. "How about we talk about your personal life for a while and leave mine alone?" he suggested, grinning. Lee's eyes closed slightly, warning him not to say anything, but Richard had the words already on his tongue. "How's the delightful Cherise Roberts doing? Have you even spoken to her since the wedding?"

Lee tossed back the last of his wine and then sat the glass down on the table. "You know Cherise avoids me every chance she gets," he pointed out. "Last week, Traci and Zack wanted us to have a family dinner at their house, but she backed out at the last minute with a lie that something came up."

Richard remembered the dinner. He had cancelled ahead of time, along with Brad, because they had other plans that night. He wished he had never gone out with Emily that night; it only encouraged her to pursue him more.

Brad didn't have any luck on his date either. The next day, his brother told him that all Alicia did was talk about Max and ways to get him to notice her more. Richard had never met Alicia, but when he did, he was going to tell her to stop leading his little brother on.

A thought passed his mind. Why was he here worrying about Brad's or Lee's love life when his was in such disarray? Dawn didn't want him any more except in a business way, and he wanted her more now than he did in the past. What was he going to do?

"Earth to Richard," Lee yelled at him from across the table.

Richard focused his attention back on his brother. "Where did you go?" Lee asked him.

"I was thinking about my future," he admitted. Lee wasn't the overly affectionate type when it came to his brothers, but he was trying to get better.

"Hey, don't worry about the restaurant or Dawn. I'll know you'll be able to keep both of them," Lee said, trying to sound encouraging.

Richard smiled at Lee. He was a little staggered by the fact that he was having such a civilized conversation with his brother. "Can you believe I'm not worried about *D4*? I'm troubled about losing Dawn to this mystery man or her leaving after she helps me save the business."

"Is this new change in you because of Dawn?" Lee asked, getting up from the table and taking his plate into the kitchen with Richard behind him. He had told the staff to leave early so they could have a long weekend. Stacking the dishes in the sink, he turned around, waiting for Richard to answer him.

"I'm still the same person," Richard answered, trying to avoid admitting to the changes he saw in himself, too.

"Sure you are," Lee replied. Folding his arms, he rested on the counter. "Why don't you want to admit that Dawn has made you feel things that you usually didn't notice?"

Richard knew that Lee was trying to trap him into saying something he didn't want to. Lee was very good at playing around with people's feelings by making them admit things they'd rather keep hidden. He wasn't going to play along with him.

"She may have helped me become more relaxed at the job, but that is it," he admitted slowly. Richard watched for any sign of disbelief to come from his brother, but he didn't get what he wanted.

"I like the little changes in you," Lee told him. "I hope they are permanent."

The conversation was going down a road that Richard wasn't ready to travel. "I better go. I have somewhere else that I have to be." He hurried from the room before Lee could stop him.

Back at his house, Richard clicked on his email to read the list Dawn had sent over. She wanted him to look into some things for her about having a different atmosphere at *D4* when it reopened. He wasn't too sure about putting all the energy into a project that might not make any sense to anyone else. He believed in working toward something with a clear end in mind. What if all the ideas and suggestions Dawn was having wouldn't work for more than a month or two? He didn't have enough money left to restart over again. This plan of hers had to work, or he was ruined.

* * * *

Wednesday morning, Richard was sitting at his desk when Dawn walked in, looking too sexy in a leopard-print skirt and black V-neck top. It brought out the richness that always surrounded her when she walked into a room. He couldn't drag his eyes away from her. "You look very nice today," he drawled, still eyeing how her legs looked in the skirt.

Dawn had an amazing pair of legs, and she wasn't even that tall.

Dawn didn't appear in the mood for Richard's flirtatious way this morning. "Thanks," she said, tossing her purse down on the table. It landed with a loud thump, showing how impatient she was becoming.

Richard didn't like the sound of Dawn's voice; it didn't possess its usual perkiness. Shoving back his chair, he got up from his desk and joined her at the table. Grasping her chin in his palm, he asked, "What took the light out of your beautiful eyes?" And then he stared into their depths, waiting for a response.

Chapter Seven

Dawn's gaze roamed Richard's face, looking for any signs of cockiness, but the only thing she saw staring back at her was concern. It broke down a little bit of the wall around her heart, causing her to answer his question. Touching his hand, she placed it back on the table. "I had a breakfast date and it didn't turn out the way I hoped," she confessed, sliding a pair of reading glasses on her face.

"What went wrong?" he asked.

The question brought her attention back to him and not the paper in front of her. Blinking, she studied him a few seconds. "Why do you want to know?" Crossing her legs, she waited for the man to her left to respond.

"We work together, and I can sense how upset you are the moment you walk through the door," Richard's deep voice said.

Dawn got lost in the sound of Richard's voice. It was so sexy, with the little drawl making it more soothing to her ears. He could never know the effect he still had on her emotions or her body. Just a few romantic words from those lips of his, and her body would be his for the taking. But with everything going on in her life, it wasn't about to happen.

Sighing softly, Dawn knew that Richard wouldn't want to be thrown into her life the way it was now, and she couldn't blame him. He was so far out of her reach, not even a good prayer would give her the dream life she wanted. "How about we stop talking about me and get back on track?"

Opening a folder, Dawn pulled two printouts for him to read. Sliding her seat next to his, she placed his copy in front of Richard, pleased that he already had his glasses on. "This is the list I emailed you about last night."

Glancing down at the list, he saw Dawn wanted to do a lot this week. "Are you sure we can get all of this done in a week?" he questioned, worried.

Taking the list back from him, Dawn marked the most important items with asterisks. She hadn't forgotten how extremely observant he was when it came to his business and the way he wanted things done. He wouldn't do something unless he knew how it was going to turn out. "I marked the suggestions we need to work on first," she told him, pointing to each one with the tip of her black pen.

* * * *

Richard still harbored some doubts because he was already having problems with connecting *D4* to the other empty building next door. His patience might not be strong enough to deal with the added pressure of anything new. Taking the pen from her hand, he wrote down a few quick notes of his own. "When do you want to start working on investing more of the money that Zack gave me?" he asked, looking at her.

"I think we should place it in a savings account in case we might need a little extra money later on."

He leaned back in the tall chair, enjoying the fire burning in Dawn's eyes. She was meant for this business; when Dawn spoke about his business, it made him feel so much closer to her. "Well, we don't have to worry about number four on the list," he said, drawing a line through it.

Frowning at him, she asked, "Why not?"

Giving Dawn a look, Richard answered her. "I don't need any more investors," he replied harshly, which meant the subject was closed to further discussion.

He wasn't about to go out and beg for more money. Didn't she realize that a man had some pride? Spinning around in the chair, Dawn moved so they were inches apart. "I don't know what gave you the idea that you don't need another investor. But get that thought out of your head," she told him, tapping her slender finger against his temple. "I'm not going to lie to you." Touching him gently on the knee, Dawn said, "After going over your books, I know you need at least one more investor for you to be able to do all the suggestions on this list."

Richard brushed Dawn's hand off his leg and jumped up from his seat. Snatching up the paper, he balled it up and tossed it across the room. "No, I don't need any more charity."

Dawn shot up out of her seat right behind him. "Don't you give me that speech," she yelled back at him.

Chapter Eight

Turning slowly, Richard looked back at Dawn, noticing how upset she was by his behavior. It wasn't like him to give up so easily, but the thought of asking another person for money made him regret even opening up *D4* in the first place. Running his fingers through his thick hair, he let off several curses before walking back over to his seat and falling back down.

"Are you positive that we can't reopen with the money that I have?" he questioned while he waited for Dawn to retake her seat.

Digging through several sheets of paper on the tabletop, Dawn searched until she found the information that she was looking for. "It took several hours of researching different sites on the Internet before I found the correct report. It points out ways to keep a new restaurant from going under, and the main suggestion is investing properly. If an owner doesn't, the business fails within the first six months."

Richard was right at his six months.

"I know you have a lot of pride, and most men do," Dawn said, trying to soothe the harsh words. "However, if you keep this up, *D4* will be nothing but a memory to you and your family. I know you don't want that." She sat back down in the chair next to him.

Hearing the truth spoken to him in such harsh terms was a blow, yet Richard knew Dawn was doing the job he hired her for. "Give me a couple of days, and I'll find another investor," he muttered with a disgusted look.

Dawn tried her best not to smile. "Don't do anything, and let me figure out something about the other investor," she told him, writing down a quick note and shoving it into her purse.

"Okay, I think we need to move on to the other thing I outlined for us to go over today," she said, taking a quick look at her watch. It was already a little past ten-thirty.

Richard didn't miss how Dawn glanced down at her watch like she did every day when it got close to lunch time. "Why are you always out of here at twelve o'clock every day?"

"I've to stay on a schedule," Dawn informed him.

He picked up on that she didn't answer his question at all, but rather gave him an excuse he didn't want to hear. "Dawn, I'm trying really hard for us to become friends while we're working together, but you aren't helping me here," he stated.

A panic seemed to set into Dawn's body. "How about we just stay the way we are and not try to make it anymore?" Dawn responded.

Richard didn't know why Dawn was denying the connection that was staring at her dead between the eyes. Sure, they had only known each other a short period of time. But they interacted so well together like they have known each other for years instead of a few short months.

This is what Zack must have felt when he laid eyes on Traci at the gym. Like his life wouldn't be complete without her in it to share it with. Why had he tossed it to the side all those months ago, when Dawn had shown such an interest in him? Now, when he wanted her, it might be too late. Focusing his attention back on the business at hand, he wanted to know exactly how long it would take to save his dream or if he should give up now.

* * * *

Dawn was surprised by how Richard wanted to give up on his restaurant. D4 could be the best establishment in Texas, but it would take long hours and sweat to make it happen. "I outlined everything on the paper. It shouldn't take more than nine months for us to get everything in place." She thought that was a good time span, yet from the way Richard was acting, it wasn't.

"Are you sure nine months isn't too long for me to be closed down?" he inquired.

The sound of the door opening drew their attention; Dawn watched the oldest and probably the best-looking of the Drace brothers walk in, with an air of authority around him. She knew several of her girlfriends would fall over themselves to make him look in their direction. If she remembered correctly, his name was Lee, and he was very outspoken.

"What brings you here?" Richard asked, standing up to give Lee a quick hug. "Do you have something to tell me?"

Dawn stood up and wondered if she should leave the room so Richard could talk to his brother in private. Something about Lee made her a little nervous, like he knew what she was thinking.

Lee glanced over Richard's shoulder at her and smiled. "Why don't you introduce me to this beautiful lady first?"

Dawn's face beamed at Lee's compliment while Richard glared at his older brother. "This is Dawn Summers. You remember she used to be manager here a few months ago."

Placing his hand in the middle of her back, Richard introduced Dawn to Lee. "Dawn, this is my oldest brother, Lee Drace."

Chapter Nine

"It's very nice to meet the woman that my brother is always talking about." Lee smiled and stuck his hand out for a handshake. "You were the main topic of several Wednesday-night dinners at my house."

Dawn stood there, a little taken aback by how blunt Richard's older brother was. She quickly shook his hand and let it go. "I'm sure that it was something bad. Richard wasn't very fond of me back then. Honestly, I don't think Richard will ever be the president of my fan club," she whispered, staring at the man she had fallen in love with two years ago.

Lee gave her a long look before he swung his gaze over to his brother. "You're right about Dawn. She is a very beautiful woman."

She was amazed at the thrill Lee's words gave her; then it vanished because she knew Richard would never say those words about her. "See…now I know you're telling a lie. Richard would never call me beautiful if his life depended on it."

"Dawn…I did tell my brother that," Richard cut in.

"Hey. I have already promised to help you reopen *D4*. You don't have to say anything you don't mean," Dawn said, making eye contact with her handsome boss. "I better go so the two of you can talk." She went around Lee and headed for the door. "It was very nice to meet you, Lee."

"Same here....Dawn," Lee answered, watching her as she strolled out the door.

* * * *

"Wow. Dawn is a knockout. I can't believe you're dating Emily over her," Lee stated, staring at Richard like he had an extra head attached.

"Why don't you worry about getting Cherise instead of Dawn?" Richard snapped back, upset that Lee was even noticing the woman he was in love with.

"I'm trying to get Cherise's attention, but she's avoiding me," Lee growled, going to sit down in a chair by Richard's desk. "You know that we have this love/hate relationship."

"Love....hate?" Richard asked, coming across the room. He rested his hip against the edge of the desk. "What? You love her and she hates you?" he joked.

"I wouldn't say I was in love with Cherise," Lee sighed. "But I do care about her."

Laughing, Richard walked around the desk and fell down into his chair. "Come off it. You're in love with Cherise Roberts. I think it was love at first sight."

"I'm not in love with Cherise, and I wish that you would stop saying that," Lee snapped, pissed that Richard was teasing him.

"Well....that's good because I heard a girl from her work is trying to hook her up on a date," Richard replied. He watched Lee's face for his reaction, and he wasn't disappointed.

Lee's eyes narrowed until they were almost slits, and his forehead covered with wrinkles. "Who in the hell is Cherise going out on a date with, and why am I just now hearing about it?"

"I thought you didn't care?" Richard asked, happy that he had something over his older brother. Lee was always the calm, collected one until it came to their sister-in-law's sister.

"Answer me, Richard," Lee hissed. "Who is the guy that Cherise thinks I'm going to let her go out on a date with?"

"I wouldn't let Cherise hear you say that. You know how she is when it comes to you bossing her around," Richard replied.

"Fine. If you won't tell me, then I'll go and ask her," Lee growled, getting up from his seat.

"Sit back down, Tarzan, and listen," Richard sighed, watching his jealous brother retake his seat. "She turned the date down." He wondered whether Lee realized that he was in love with Cherise, no matter how much he tried to deny it. He definitely wanted to be around when the truth hit Lee in the face. He didn't know who was in worse trouble, Lee or Cherise.

"Do you know why she turned the date down?" Lee asked, reaching for a peppermint inside a glass jar on Richard's desk. Opening it, Lee popped it inside his mouth.

"No, Zack didn't tell me all of that. All he knew was a guy's wife at Cherise's job was trying to fix her up with one of her single friends," he answered, watching Lee bite down on the soft candy.

"Good. I'm glad she said no because I would hate to make a surprise visit to her house," Lee said around the candy in his mouth. "If she's going on a date with anyone, it's going to be me."

"Are you sure about that?" Richard questioned, surprised by the determination in Lee's voice. He had never seen his brother this passionate about a woman before. What was so special about Cherise that she made his brother act like this?

"I'm positive, and that's all I have to say," Lee said, swallowing down the last of the candy in his mouth. "Now that we have spent some time talking about me, how about we talk about you? How are you going to get Miss Summers to realize that you want more than an employer and employee relationship with her? She doesn't seem too certain about moving your relationship forward."

"I think I really did some damage to Dawn, the way I treated her before she quit D4. Back then, I would catch her looking at me when she didn't think I was looking. Or maybe twice a day, she would find little ways to be near me, and I didn't appreciate her attention when I had it," Richard complained. "Now all she does is come to work, and we sit at that table and work on financial stuff for the restaurant, and I hate it. I stare at her now more than she looks at me. Sometimes I think I don't have a chance in hell at making her feel anything for me any more." Richard hated to think that after D4 was up and running, Dawn could be out of his life.

"Do you think if one of us talked to her, she might let something slip?" Lee inquired.

"No. She has already run into you and Brad; that's enough. I don't want Zack interfering with my love life. Anyways, he needs to focus his attention on Traci and the baby."

"Yeah, I was really happy when he told me about the baby. It's going to be so nice to have our first niece or nephew around. The way we were going, I thought none of us was ever going to get married and raise a family."

"I always thought I might be the first one to get married," Richard confessed. "Zack falling in love first and taking the big walk down the aisle took me by surprise. But after seeing Zack and Traci together now, it was meant to be."

"So who were you going to marry? Emily?" Lee taunted.

"Yes…. I'm going to marry Emily," Richard tossed back.

* * * *

"Oh…I'm sorry I didn't mean to interrupt," Dawn whispered from the doorway as she stared back and forth between Richard and Lee. She wouldn't let Richard see how her heart was breaking at the news about his upcoming marriage to Emily. She didn't have any right to be jealous. Richard hadn't been in her life for a while, and when he was, he couldn't stand the sight of her.

"I forgot my notebook and came back to get it." She rushed over to the table and picked up the pad as Richard was coming around his desk to her.

"Dawn...wait. Let me explain about what you heard." Richard's deep voice pleaded with her, but she kept going out the door and closed it behind her. She couldn't let him see the tears in her eyes.

Chapter Ten

Richard cursed under his breath and was racing for the door after Dawn when a hand wrapped around his arm and stopped him. Jerking his arm away, he glared over his shoulder at his brother. "What in the hell do you think you're doing?" he yelled. "I need to find Dawn and make her understand what she overheard wasn't true." He started for the door again, only to be pulled back by Lee.

"Let her go," Lee said "Dawn isn't in the right mind to listen to you right now."

"What are you talking about, 'don't go after her'?" Richard snapped. He spun around and faced his brother. Sometimes he didn't understand the thoughts that came into his brother's head. He couldn't let Dawn think he was going to marry clingy Emily.

"You heard what I said. Dawn needs time to calm down, and you'll be able to explain yourself later," Lee exclaimed, going back over to his chair and sitting back down. "Do you think if you follow right at this moment, she would give you the time of day?"

Richard stared at the closed door. The need to chase after Dawn was strong, but Lee was right. She wouldn't talk to him now if her life depended on it. Walking back over to his desk, Richard fell back down into his chair and wondered how he was going to get out of this mess.

"Dawn is going to make sure that our relationship is strictly business now," he sighed, already guessing the excuses Dawn would use to avoid spending any extra time with him. "She thought I was a jerk before. I just cemented my feet with that conversation."

"She doesn't think you're a jerk," Lee cut in. "If she did, Dawn wouldn't have gotten that devastated look on her face. She still has feelings for you and doesn't want you to know it."

Richard wished that he could get Lee to leave so he could have a few minutes to himself and work over in his mind what just happened. Dawn was so sensitive about things, and this might have just sent her running so far away nothing would bring her back.

"You look like you need to be alone, so I'm going to leave." Lee stood up from his seat and stared at him. "Don't forget tonight is Wednesday. I expect to see you at dinner tonight—and without Emily."

He couldn't believe his brother brought that up after the day he had been having. "I didn't bring her there last time. You know that she followed me from work and invited herself."

"Yeah, I know but I couldn't resist throwing that in...for me." Lee laughed as he went to the door. After he stopped laughing, his brother opened the door and then paused and looked back at him.

"Don't let what happened today with Dawn get to you. She seems like a person of her word. If nothing else, she'll be back to help you save the restaurant." Lee gave him a wave and then went out the door.

"Lee, I hope you're right, but I don't have a good feeling about my future with Miss Dawn Summers at all," Richard groaned as he rested his head back on his leather chair.

* * * *

Dawn tossed her car keys on the table as soon as the front door closed behind her. Why in the world was she still in love with a man who was not in love with her? When would she get it through her head that Richard Drace didn't want her? If she was a bottle of open honey and he was a bee, he wouldn't come close enough to sample her sweet taste.

Kicking her shoes off, she walked around her empty house and wondered how she was going to get through the next several weeks, day in and day out, sitting next to Richard. She wouldn't let herself fantasize about a man who was no longer free. He was marrying Emily. Just the thought of the younger girl's name made her want to cry. With her body and perfect face, she could have been a regular on *Baywatch*. There was no way she could or should have to compete with that.

Padding around the living room in her bare feet, she remembered how excited she had been about working with Richard again. Every morning before she got out of her car at *D4*, she secretly hoped Richard would tell her what a huge mistake he had made by tossing her away.

"You need to stop wanting something to happen that never will," Dawn scolded herself as she made her way back to her bedroom. "Richard has shown you time and time again who he wants, and it isn't you, sister girl."

Inside her peach and cream bedroom, Dawn tossed her body in the oversized chair by her bed and let the events of the day finally take over her body. Before she knew what had happened, she was fast asleep with the gorgeous face of Richard Drace haunting her dreams.

* * * *

"Have you heard the news?" Lee asked before he took a bite of his grilled salmon.

"What news?" Zack asked, dragging his eyes away from his wife.

"No, I haven't heard the news, either," Brad chimed in, staring at Lee from the far end of the table.

"Neither have we," Traci answered, looking at Cherise, then back at him.

"You better not tell them what I think you're going to tell them," Richard growled at his oldest brother from his seat by his sister-in-law, Cherise.

Lee gave Richard a wicked grin before he wiped his mouth with a napkin and then placed it beside his plate. "Richard and Emily are getting married."

"What?" The other two Drace brothers yelled, swinging their gazes from Lee over to a pissed Richard.

"I thought he was in love with Dawn," Traci whispered, her eyes still on Lee.

"So did I," Cherise interjected, without looking in Lee's direction.

"Don't listen to him," Richard exclaimed, interrupting his thoughts.

"Why shouldn't they listen to me?" Lee questioned. "Isn't that what you were telling me when Dawn walked in your office?"

"You know I was being a smart-ass when I said that to you," Richard snapped. "You also know that I sure in the hell didn't want Dawn to hear that."

Lee shrugged one of his shoulders. "Maybe I did know you didn't mean it, but you have been doing that a lot lately."

"A lot of what?" Richard questioned. "I don't have a clue what you're talking about."

"Saying things in the heat of the moment, then regretting them the second they left the tip of your tongue."

"Lee does have a point there," Brad agreed. "You about tore my head off at the office the other day when I walked in on you and Dawn pressed together."

"Richard did the same thing to me, too," Zack tossed out. "He hated that I came for lunch because he just had a fight with Dawn."

Richard couldn't believe his family that supposedly loved him was talking to him like he was a stranger on the street. He came to this dinner tonight so he could get some moral support from them, not get turned over the coals.

Chapter Eleven

Dawn rested her head against the steering wheel and counted slowly to ten. She couldn't believe he wouldn't give it back to her. For the past four weeks, she had been meeting with him, and he promised that today would be the day he would place it in her hand. How in the hell could she keep concentrating on helping Richard when her own life was falling apart?

She was already in big trouble with Richard because she hadn't shown up for work for the past two days. He had called and left so many messages that she lost count after the tenth. Did she truly think she wanted to be around while he planned his wedding to Emily? Hell, that damn girl was barely a step above stupid, at best.

She'd bet her last dollar Emily wasn't in love with Richard, but with the idea of dating a restaurant owner. It didn't matter that *D4* was in a bit of trouble right now. It wouldn't last long, and Emily was smart enough to realize that, too.

Lifting her head off the steering wheel, Dawn pushed her sunglasses on top of her head, grabbed her purse off the seat beside her, and got out of the car. She had better go face the music with Richard. After her no-show for the past forty-eight hours, her pink slip was probably already waiting for her anyway.

Walking into D4, Dawn couldn't help but stop and look at the beauty of the place. Tables ran the length of the building, making a total of twenty-four for the whole restaurant. Pure white linens covered the tables, with sterling silver utensils on each of the tables. She had told Richard several times to box the stuff up until he reopened the place, but he told her no. He thought if anything got boxed up, it meant that his dreams failed, and he wasn't ready to admit defeat.

The way he fell in love with something and held on with both hands was the quality she admired the most about him. No matter how hard the object struggled, he wasn't about to let go until he proved that he was the winner.

"Who have you been with the last two days that you couldn't show up for work?" Richard's slight drawl sent the familiar shiver through her body, stopping at her stomach.

Spinning around, she was shocked to see Richard wearing a hunter green t-shirt, well-worn jeans that fit him in all the right places with a pair of tennis shoes. He looked more like a college jock than a thirty-two-year-old man. Damn, her heart and body weren't ready for this.

"I apologize for not calling in the two days I was gone, but who I was with isn't any of your business," Dawn replied.

"Yes, it is my business when the woman I'm paying to save my business isn't doing her job. If I wanted to hire a half-ass person to show up when they wanted, I could have given the job to Emily," Richard snapped.

Dawn was so proud of herself when she remained emotionless when Richard mentioned his fiancée's name. Why would he want her here when he could have his twenty-three-year-old playmate? Hell, she must be over the hill to him at the ripe old age of twenty-nine.

"You know what? You're right. Why would you want me here when Emily could do so much of a better job?" she snapped back, tired of Richard's constant attacks on her. She was still in love with him, but she had too much going on to deal with him now. "How about we forget we ever met again, and you hire Emily or whoever else you want instead of me!"

She turned to leave when Richard stepped into her path. "Move out of my way."

"No, I don't want anyone else. I only want you," he whispered, staring into her eyes.

If only that was true, Dawn thought, trying not to fall in love with Richard more than she already was.

* * * *

Richard felt his usual panic setting in when he thought Dawn might leave again. He might not be lucky enough to find her a second time. These past two days had been so hard on him. He still needed to explain that what she had heard about Emily was a lie. How could he want any other woman in his bed or life but her? However, Dawn didn't seem too eager to talk to him at the moment. Her eyes had a spark to them that he never noticed before, and a surge of jealousy hit in hard in the chest. He would find out what was going on with her; it didn't matter how long it would take. But first he needed to clear the air about Emily, or Dawn was out of here.

"I'm not marrying Emily," he confessed. "What you heard was a mistake."

"What happened? Did you not buy her the new trinket that she wanted?" she questioned. "I don't have time to be pulled into the life of the young yet restless Emily. She's your girlfriend, so why are you always telling me about her?" Dawn asked, jealous of the woman who had what she wanted more than anything in this world.

Richard tried to keep the smile off his face but couldn't. Dawn was jealous! If she was jealous of Emily, that meant only one thing; she had feelings for him. He hadn't totally messed up his chances with the breathtaking woman in front of him.

"First, Emily isn't my girlfriend, and she never has been my girlfriend. She's a splinter deep in my finger that I can't get rid of," Richard retorted, watching Dawn's face for a reaction. He was pleased when a small smile touched the corner of her full lips.

"She wouldn't like that you compared her to a piece of wood," Dawn replied.

"Emily's likes aren't my concern," he answered, reaching out to run his finger along Dawn's perfect jawbone. He almost danced for joy when she didn't move back from his touch. "I'm only worried about you leaving before D4 is up and running."

Richard watched the happiness leave Dawn's face as she brushed his hand away from her face.

"You don't have to worry. I'll keep my promise. I won't leave *D4* until it's back at the top like before."

He watched Dawn headed toward his office. What in the hell did he say wrong this time? What words did she want to hear from him? Didn't he just tell her that he didn't want Emily? Who else could he possibly want besides her? Maybe he was going about this all wrong. Dawn paid way too much attention to the words that came out of his mouth and that got him into trouble. It was time for him to do something new to make her understand she was the woman he wanted.

Richard hurried behind Dawn and closed the office door behind them, locking it to make sure that they didn't get interrupted like the last four times. "Dawn, wait. There's something I want to do before we get started."

Dawn tossed her purse down at their usual table in the middle of the room and pulled out that red notebook he was getting used to. "What is it?" she sighed, turning to study him.

He strolled across the room until he took up every inch of her space and she didn't have anywhere to move. "This," he whispered before he pulled her body to his and planted a hot kiss on her surprised mouth.

Dawn struggled in his arms for a few seconds before she wrapped her arms around his neck and snuggled closer. His body leaped to attention, and he pressed his erection into her stomach while his tongue mated with hers.

Richard knew that if he died right at the moment, he would die a happy man. The woman he cared about more than anything in the world was wrapped tight in his arms, kissing him with the same burning passion he felt for her.

* * * *

I shouldn't let myself be this weak for him, Dawn thought as Richard's tongue continued to stroke the inside of her mouth. This wasn't supposed to be happening. She only came back to work for him, not make out with him in the middle of the day. Her body started to tremble as Richard's fingers stroked the sides of her breasts. Why wasn't she stronger when it came to this man? What was it about him that made her want to melt into a pool at his gorgeous feet?

Did she really have enough strength to stay away around from him and *D4* after all of this was over? She didn't have a choice. She had to make Richard a part of her past the second this restaurant reopened its doors.

"No," she moaned, twisting her mouth away from Richard's firm lips. "We are breaking one of the rules we agreed on."

"Haven't you heard that rules are meant to be broken?" Richard asked, jerking her back into his arms.

"We can't afford to break any of the rules. We need all our attention on the big picture," she complained, trying to pry Richard's hands off her waist. Hell, why did he have to smell so good? It was making her resisting him so much harder.

"I am thinking about the big picture," Richard breathed by her ears, as his hands slid underneath her blouse, his thighs pressed her hips against the table. There was no mistaking the thick cock in the front of his pants.

Chapter Twelve

"You know that isn't the big picture I was talking about," Dawn breathed by the corner of his mouth, as her hips wiggled against his.

Richard didn't want the picture Dawn was talking about. All he wanted to do was keep her in his arms like this forever. He had said so many things to her over the past few weeks that he was lucky she didn't slap him when he kissed her.

"Have dinner with me," he asked, easing her body back from his while his fingers stroked her back underneath her blouse.

"That wouldn't be a good idea," Dawn replied.

"Why not?" he questioned, playing with the clasp on her bra. How could he learn more about her if she didn't want to see him outside the restaurant?

"Is this going to be a business dinner?" she questioned, removing his hands from her shirt and pulling it back down. "That's the only way I'll be able to have dinner with you."

"No, it wouldn't be a business dinner," Richard said. "You know that I was asking you out on a real date." He couldn't let her find a reason to say no to him. Dawn had let him kiss her again and that was the first step he had accomplished to winning her heart back.

"Why would we have anything more than a business dinner?" she questioned. Dawn placed her hand in the middle of his chest and tried to shove him out of the way, but he didn't move.

"If you have to ask that after the hot kiss we just shared, then I'm more out of practice than I thought," he teased, hoping to get a smile. "Did you not enjoy it?"

"You know I did," Dawn admitted, running her fingers across his mouth. "That's why it can't happen again. We aren't supposed to be in a relationship."

He caught Dawn's wandering fingers and laid them over his beating heart. He didn't like the turn this conversation was taking. "Who am I supposed to be with, then, if it isn't you?" Dawn opened her mouth, and he quickly raised his free hand to silence her. "I don't want to hear the name Emily come out of your mouth. I don't want that girl, and I never did."

"When did that change?" Dawn questioned, moving his hand out of her face. "You're always making it a competition between the two of us."

"I never thought Emily would take two dates that seriously," he answered, glad that Dawn was talking to him instead of running off.

"You've been out on two dates with her?" Dawn exclaimed. "Well, you must had something in common to see her a second time."

Richard cursed under his breath. What was it with him that he was always sticking his foot in his mouth when it came to Dawn? He never let the words come from his lips that he wanted her to hear.

He would never end up giving her the ring he wanted to if this kept up.

"Emily forced those two dates on me by giving me some pitiful story, so I would take her out to eat." He searched Dawn's doubtful face with his eyes. She had to believe that he didn't want any other woman over her. "Kitten, I'll tell you again and again until you believe me. I don't want Emily in my life." Richard brushed a soft kiss over Dawn's moist lips. "I only want to get to know you better so you'll stop thinking I'm a first-class jerk all the time. Won't you let me prove how good I could be for you?"

"I don't think you're a first-class jerk," Dawn admitted, staring into his eyes.

"Good….at least I don't have that hanging over my head." He grinned, but it faded when he heard Dawn's next words.

"But that doesn't mean I'm saying yes to a romantic dinner with you," Dawn confessed, sliding around his body. "We should stick to the rules we made the first day I agreed to come back to work for you."

Richard didn't know if he was coming or going when it came to the woman trying to shove her feelings for him inside a box. He wouldn't let her get this far with him, only to back out now. He wanted to see Dawn in a sexy dress, and he always got what he wanted out of life.

"Baby, those rules went out the door the first time I stuck my tongue in your mouth," he said, moving to stand behind Dawn. Grabbing a fistful of hair, he eased it off her neck. "You know you want to say yes….so why don't you?" he breathed by her ear.

Dawn tried to shake off his hold, but he wasn't having any of that. He craved this woman in front of him with urgency he never experienced before. He had been dumb enough to let her escape once; it wasn't about to happen a second time. "I can promise you that you'll have a good time." Richard ran the tip of his tongue alongside the shell of Dawn's ear.

"No…I can't do it," Dawn whispered, shaking her head.

"Why not?" he groaned, spinning Dawn around to face him. "Do you think I'm going to do something to hurt you?" It would kill him if she thought that.

"Yes…I think you will say something to hurt me," Dawn confessed. "You always toss an insult at me when your back gets against the wall."

Richard cursed himself again a thousand times as Dawn's words struck a chord in his heart. He never knew how much his words cut at her. He had a lot to make up for, but he had an underlying fear he might be out of chances with Dawn.

"Give me a chance to redeem myself in your eyes," he begged. "I can prove to you that your love won't be wasted on me."

Shoving him in the chest, Dawn stumbled back from him, her eyes wide with shock. "What makes you think I'm in love with you?" she choked out.

He didn't get a good feeling from the way Dawn was staring at him. It was almost like he guessed her most guarded secret. Hell, he told her before she left six months ago that he knew what her feelings were for him. Wait a minute! Had Dawn changed her mind about him? Was there really someone else in her life now? Was that the person she was always meeting with for lunch?

Hell, no! He wouldn't let another man steal Dawn from him. Not after he finally realized how much he loved her. What if she already had a man sharing her bed? Richard gave his head a quick shake. *NO!* He wouldn't let that thought enter his mind.

"I just know that you are," Richard said, stroking the sides of Dawn's arms with his fingers. He could touch her forever and never get tired. "If you give me a chance, I'll let you know how I feel about you too, Kitten."

* * * *

Dawn really wanted to believe the words Richard was trying to tell her, but she had opened her heart to him so many times, only to have it crushed by him time and time again. Was she strong enough to give him another chance? Richard was everything she had ever wanted in a man, but the way he kept Emily on the side still bothered her. Did she want to chance her heart on a maybe?

"I'll give you two weeks," she agreed, throwing caution to the wind in hopes that she wasn't doing the wrong thing.

"No…I don't think that will work," Richard said matter-of-factly, while his fingers slid down to cup her butt.

She tried not to think about how good his hands felt on her body. "Why won't it work?" Dawn gasped as Richard's hands massaged her ass through her jeans.

"The things that I want to do to this sinful body of yours can't be done in two weeks. Shit, it can't be done in a month." His husky voice broke as his rough tongue stroked the side of her neck. "I want you….no, I crave you for the next two months in my life and in my bed."

Dawn's body shivered as hot, blissful images of herself in Richard's bed came into her mind. She couldn't believe she was standing here, letting him talk to her like this. There had to be some law against one man having this much sex appeal. "Two months," she groaned as Richard's fingers continued to stroke her body. "I can't give you two months."

"Why not?" he growled, separating their bodies to stare down at her face. "Are you saying that you're already seeing someone else? Well, it doesn't matter. As of this moment, you're mine." Wrapping his hand in her hair, Richard brought her face within a breath of his. "And I didn't share my toys as a child, so I'm in the hell not going to share my woman," he growled, then planted a long, searching kiss on her mouth.

Dawn didn't know how long she stayed wrapped in Richard's arms, but when he finally pulled away, there was a light in his eyes that would have scared the most seasoned woman.

"I'm not your woman," Dawn whispered past her swollen lips. She wouldn't let Richard's sweet words sway her. He just wanted to explore the attraction that was burning between the two of them. She craved the same thing, so why deny what they both were feeling?

* * * *

God, he had a long way to go with Dawn, but he wasn't about to give up. He wouldn't rush things with her. A part of Dawn still didn't completely trust him, and he understood why, but he would do everything in his power to change that in the next two months.

"How about we put this conversation on the back burner until another day?" Richard moved away from Dawn. He went over to the door and unlocked it. "Now, what other ideas has that pretty little head come up with to help me?" he asked, resting his back against the door.

Dawn's hazel eyes were bright as she stared back at him. "Are you sure you want to explore this instead of what we were just doing?"

Her raspy voice sent the blood rushing from his head straight down to the hard-on already swelling back to life in his pants. Shit, did Dawn realize how hot her words just sounded to him? If they were anywhere else but *D4*, he would take her up on that offer.

"How about you ask me that again when we aren't here?" he requested, pushing his back away from the door. "I promise you'll love my answer," Richard whispered, stopping in front of the woman who had stolen his heart.

"I can't ask you that again," Dawn sighed, taking a step back. "It took enough for me to say it the first time," she stated, searching his face with her eyes. "I had to prepare myself for your rejection because I'm used to you denying any attraction you may have towards me."

"Kitten, haven't you heard a word I've said?" he asked, wanting Dawn to really hear his words and believe them. "I care about you more than I have any other woman. I want you to be able to ask me anything, no matter what it is."

"Maybe later after we finish going over my new notes," Dawn said, smiling at him.

Richard froze by the door as he watched Dawn pull out a chair and take a seat at the table. She had never smiled at him like that before, so open and carefree. Even the whiteness of her smile was breathtaking. He didn't know if he could spend the rest of the day next to her without kissing her mouth.

Don't move too fast and scare her away. She's beginning to trust you a little; don't ruin it by saying something stupid, he thought as he headed over to the table. "Kitten, are you ready to hold my future in your small hands?" Richard asked as he sat down at the table.

Dawn glanced up from the paper she was reading and stared at him, and then a cute grin overtook her features. "Keep talking like that, and I might start to believe you have real feelings for me."

His hand shot out and wrapped around Dawn's upper arm; then he pulled her until her shoulder touched his chest. "Woman…my feelings for you are more than real. They are hot and heavy. I can't think straight the second your perfect body walks into the room. I'm not going to read another piece of paper or sign another damn check until I make you believe me."

Richard could tell from the way her eyes kept glancing away from his that Dawn still didn't believe him. "What do I have to say or do to make you understand I'm not lying to you?"

Dawn slid her arm out of his grip. "Time…I just need time. I have a lot of other things going on in my life right now, and I don't know if I've the extra energy for you."

"Other things…is that a woman's code for another man?"

Chapter Thirteen

Dawn couldn't believe the attitude that Richard was giving her and the conclusions that he was jumping to. She never once mentioned another man in her life, and hell, if she did have one there wasn't anything that he could do about it.

"I'm not seeing another man, but I do have some personal things I need to take care of," she confessed. "I can't get involved in a deep relationship with anyone until I get this worked out."

Richard moved away from her and sat back in his chair. "What are you hiding from me? Did something happen to you those six months you were gone away from me?" His eyes bore into her like he was trying to read all the secrets on her soul.

"I really don't want to talk about this." Dawn sat back in her chair. She glanced down at her watch and was surprised that it was a little after twelve o'clock. She was late. She jumped up from the table and snatched her purse off the floor. "I have to go. I'm late for a lunch date." Dawn rushed out the door before Richard could stop her.

* * * *

Richard got up from his seat and rushed to the door but stopped before he went completely out. He wanted to follow Dawn so badly and find out why she left every day for lunch, but she had already told him that she didn't need his help. He didn't know how to handle these hot and cold feelings that Dawn kept throwing his way.

He needed someone to talk to about this because with the way things were going, Dawn wouldn't be in his life after D4 was up and running. Checking to make sure that his car keys were in his pocket, Richard left and hoped Dawn would be here when he got back.

* * * *

"I can't believe you came to see me with your woman problems. I'm not the usual Drace that everyone goes to for relationship advice," Brad said, wiping the sweat from his face with a towel wrapped around his neck.

"You are the only one who will understand the dilemma I'm going through," Richard sighed, sitting on the bench beside his younger brother. He glanced at the couples playing tennis on the court in front of them. Tennis was never his favorite pastime, but Brad had loved it ever since the age of three. "Do you think you can help me?" he asked, looking back at his brother.

"I might be able to help you if I knew exactly what the problem was," Brad replied, tossing his damp towel into the duffel bag by his feet.

"I need to learn how to block out the hurt from when the woman you care about doesn't feel the same way about you."

"Why are you coming to me wanting advice about that?"

"Why shouldn't I come to you? You're the expert in Unrequited Love 101. You have been in love with Alicia for the past two years, haven't you?" Richard answered.

Brad snatched his gym bag off the ground and stood up. "Funny, Rich. I thought you came to me for help, not to piss me off."

Richard grabbed his brother by the arm and yanked him back down to the bench next to him. "Sorry. I don't mean to insult you, but you have wanted Alicia for a while now."

"What about Lee? Hasn't he been in love with Cherise for a while, too? Why aren't you pushing your useless advice on him?" Brad questioned.

"Unlike you, Lee is going after the woman that he wants. Cherise is the one who's fighting what she feels for our brother, but I believe Lee is wearing her down," Richard mused. "But enough about everyone else. I want to talk about us."

"From what you just told me, I won't be much help to you because I can't make Alicia fall in love with me," Brad complained. "What should I do, hit her over the head and drag her back to my cave?"

Richard turned on the bench and faced his brother. "I have an idea that just might work to help you land Alicia's heart, but you need to help me first."

Brad's eyes lit up. "Can you really help me with her? You know that she believes she's in love with Max. Plus any time I try to get some free time with her, he always shows up."

He placed his hand on his brother's shoulder. "I promise I have a plan for you. Now will you help me?"

"Fine…what can I do to help you?" Brad sighed, knocking his hand off his shoulder.

Richard glanced around to make sure no one on the tennis court or the other benches was paying any attention to him. "Now, hear me out before you say no to my suggestion. I know this will work if I get your help."

"Either tell me, or I'm outta here," Brad groaned, reaching for his bag again. "I don't have time for this. Alicia is taking me out to dinner to tell me about her new assignment at the news station."

He opened his mouth to ask whether Max was going to be anywhere in the vicinity, because that would be the only reason Alicia would treat Brad to dinner.

"Don't you know that you've the worst poker face?" Brad growled next to him. "Stop thinking the worst about Alicia, or I won't help you. You may not believe it, but I know she has feelings for me."

Richard wanted to argue, but how could he? Wasn't he trying to find a way to get Dawn to notice him? She told him that she wanted more time. He didn't know how much more time he could give to her. He wanted to announce to his brothers that he had found the love of his life, but that would have Dawn running for the door.

"Sorry. I shouldn't judge your feelings for Alicia when I feel the same way about Dawn. So, bro, what are we going to do?" he asked.

"Fight for the women that we love until they realize how much they love us, too," Brad answered. "Now why don't you tell me what you want me to do with Dawn?"

"You're not going to do one damn thing with Dawn," Richard corrected with a low growl. "You're going to help me find out what she's doing every day during her lunch break."

"You want me to follow her?" Brad sputtered, clearly shocked by his question.

He didn't want a lecture from Brad. Dawn didn't want to tell him what she was up to, so he would just find out on his own. "Don't make it sound so malevolent. You only have to find out what's she hiding from me."

Brad grabbed his bag off the ground and leaped off the bench, away from him. "No way. I'm not doing anything like that at all. Why don't you just ask her what is going on?"

Richard got off the bench behind his brother and blocked Brad's path as he started to walk away. "Don't you think I've done that already? Dawn is tight-lipped as a clam."

Swinging the duffel bag on his shoulder, Brad's jaw clenched, and his left eyebrow twitched a little. "All I have to do is find out what's she's doing on her lunch break, and that's it?"

He smiled at his now favorite brother. "Yes...that's all I want you to do for me. Dawn is so secretive now."

"I'll do it on one condition."

"What?" Richard mumbled.

"Make Lee and Zack stop talking bad about Alicia. She's the woman I want to be with, and I won't stop until I get her," Brad promised, staring him dead in the eye.

Who did Brad think he was, a miracle worker? "I'll try my best."

"I don't want your best. I want you to tell them to back off and let me live my life," Brad retorted. "Or I won't help you with Dawn."

Richard stared at Brad with complete surprise on his face. He had never heard Brad stand up to him or any of the other brothers like this. "I'll have a talk with the both of them as soon as I finish up here."

"Good. After you're finished with them, meet me at my house, and we can discuss what you want me to do about Dawn." Brad told him goodbye and left his brother standing on the tennis court.

* * * *

Dawn took a sip of her drink and waited for her lunch date to arrive. Placing the ginger ale back on the table, she wished now that she had asked for something stronger. How much longer did she have to deal with Johnny? Shit, he was calling her every day now, no matter how many times she told him not to. Why did she go back to him for help after the fight with Richard? He always acted like he was going to help her, but he always made her problem worse.

"Hey, sweet thing, have you been waiting for me long?" Johnny snickered, falling down into the seat in front of her.

The scent of cheap cologne and unwashed clothes burned her nose. "How did they let you in here smelling like that?" she whispered, holding up a napkin to her nose.

Johnny looked around and then leaned across the table. "I snuck in while the hostess was seating another couple," he confessed, falling back against the seat.

She watched as a handful of dirt fell off Johnny's shoulder and hit the thick tan carpet that was throughout the restaurant. "Are you ready to deal now?"

"'Deal' or 'no deal' are the only words that are going to come out of my mouth, luscious lips," Johnny whispered, leering at her mouth. "Damn, you always did have the best pair of lips. Has Richard sampled them yet?"

She dropped the napkin back down on the table and yanked her checkbook out of her purse. "Name the price that you want so I can get that tape. I want you out of my life."

Johnny smiled, showing a mouthful of discolored and missing teeth. She was still stunned how drugs had taken him down in the past couple of months. "Now, don't go getting all high and mighty on me. Who was there for you when you needed help?" he yelled, drawing attention to their table.

"I'm sorry. Keep your voice down," Dawn muttered.

Johnny winked at her. Picking up her drink, he drained the glass and then set it back on the table, leaving black fingerprints all over the glass. "You need to learn how to respect me, girl. I know you think you're all Miss Upper Crust now because of your job, but I still remember the Dawn from the trailer park."

"How can you say that? Didn't I bring you out here with me when I moved? Remember how you promised to change your life but didn't?" Dawn snapped, tired of Johnny's constant whining.

"You seem to be leaving out how you left me at the shelter and moved on to bigger and better things, like that Richard Drace," Johnny tossed back. "We were supposed to be a team, but you dumped me the second you got the chance."

"Johnny, that is the past, and there isn't a thing I can do about it, but I can help you now," she said, trying to get through to a drug-crazed brain.

"Don't talk to me like I'm beneath you, Dawn," Johnny demanded. "I haven't shot up or taken a pill in two days. I wanted my mind clear so I could deal with you."

Dawn didn't believe Johnny's story because he was a classic dope head. He didn't know how to go two days without taking something. She remembered one time he wanted to get high so bad that he drank a bottle of cough syrup.

"How much do you want for that tape?" she asked, opening up her checkbook.

"I don't know if you have enough me to buy it back from me," Johnny taunted, running his blackened fingers on the white tablecloth. "I might get more money if I place it on the Internet and charge to see it."

The pen dropped from her hand with a loud thump. "You can't do that. Richard might see it and hate me."

Johnny shrugged, and another pile of dirt fell on the floor around his chair. "That's not my problem. You were the one who wanted to make extra money."

"Please don't do this to me. I thought we were friends," Dawn pleaded above the sound of her breaking heart.

"Hey, I didn't make you go into that place and do those things. I only told you about the place. So for my silence and the only copy of the tape, I want two hundred and fifty thousand dollars," Johnny sneered.

Dawn picked up her pen and checkbook, placing them back in her purse. "You know that I don't have that kind of money."

Smirking, Johnny stood up and ran his finger through his long, stringy hair. "Well, I guess it's no deal then." He winked at her before he strolled from the restaurant under the disgusted eyes of the other customers.

"Shit, what in the hell am I going to do now?" Dawn cried, dropping her head down on the tablecloth.

Chapter Fourteen

"Hey, you look like you just lost your best friend," Richard teased, walking into his brother's office as he closed the door behind him. "What's wrong?"

Lee pitched his pen down on his desk and then ran his hands down his face. "I don't know what I'm going to do with her. One minute I hate her with a passion, and in the next breath, I want to kiss her senseless until she admits that she wants me."

"I take it you're talking about our sister-in-law's sister." Richard grinned, pausing in front of his brother's desk.

"Don't stand there grinning at me. Sit down and tell me why you're here," Lee barked.

"If you going to be an asshole, I can go," Richard hissed, turning to leave. He didn't have time for Lee's mood after the lecture Brad gave him at the tennis court.

"Sit your ass down and tell me what you want," Lee sighed

Hiding his grin, he spun back around and fell down into the chair. "What makes you think I want anything from you?" he asked, relaxing in his seat. When *D4* was back up and running, he was going to buy two of these chairs for his office. They would be killer to make love in with Dawn.

"I know you, Richard."

"Fine…I want you to stop picking on Brad about Alicia. He cares about her, and we need to respect his feelings."

"Why are you defending Brad to me?" Lee grilled. "Has he gotten something over on you?"

Brad *owed* him big time for this. He better find out who Dawn was seeing on her lunch breaks. "No, he doesn't have anything over me. I just was thinking it's about time we start treating him like the adult that he is."

"He isn't acting like an adult, chasing around a woman who doesn't want him," Lee complained. "Brad is a good-looking guy, and he could get any woman he wanted. Why does he continue to waste his time with Alicia?"

"The same reason you keep pursuing Cherise: because he's in love with her."

"You can't compare Cherise to Alicia. Cherise is a strong-willed woman who's fighting her feelings for me. You've seen how she looks at me during the family dinners. I've seen the desire in her eyes. I only need to make her realize I'm not the enemy. Alicia doesn't want our brother."

After hearing Lee, Richard wanted to fight for Brad and Alicia even more. "We can't say how she feels about Brad because we have never met her. How about I tell Brad to invite her to dinner next week?" he suggested.

"How will that help anything?"

Richard couldn't believe Lee was being so obstinate about this. "It will show that Brad we support him and want to know more about the woman he's interested in."

Lee gave his head a quick shake. "No, I don't think that's a good idea."

Crossing his legs, Richard fell back against the seat. He knew one thing that would get Lee to say yes. "I'm sure that having more people at dinner next week will make Cherise say yes to an invitation. How long has it been since she has stepped foot in your house?"

"Three weeks," Lee growled. "Fine, let Brad invite Alicia, and tell him that I'll be on my best behavior."

Richard stood up from his seat and chuckled. "You can't talk about Brad. You're just as bad when it comes to Cherise."

"Don't piss me off, or I'll change my mind about dinner," Lee hissed, but Richard could see the laughter in his brother's eyes.

"No, you won't, because you want a chance to see Cherise and steal a kiss or two," Richard replied, making his way towards the door. "You want this dinner to happen as much as Brad—maybe more, big brother," he taunted before going out the door.

* * * *

Sitting behind Richard's desk, Dawn typed in the things she wanted to start working on next week to help rebuild D4. She needed to start earning more money, so Johnny wouldn't place that tape of her on the Internet for the entire world to see. How could she have been so dumb as to do something like that?

119

She had to work fast and get the money. Because after talking to Johnny again, he gave her one month to get it, or she wouldn't have a second chance.

Bringing her attention back to the computer monitor, she typed in the rest of the agenda she wanted Richard to follow while she worked on finding a way to redo the layout of *D4*.

Determine new menu prices.

Purchase new equipment to replace the older models.

Develop a floor plan.

Select the new décor for *D4*.

Work on a service system.

Plan if you want live entertainment or a dance floor

Hire a new staff.

Advertise aggressively.**

Decide if you want breakfast and lunch between 7:00-3:00 or dinner from 3:00-8:00.

Liquor license.

"Do you really expect me to be able to do all those things on your list in a month?" The deep timbre of Richard's voice drawled by her ear before he planted a kiss on her cheek, sending a shiver down her spine.

Hitting the save button first, Dawn spun around in her chair, and her heart caught in her throat at the gentle look in Richard's eyes. "I didn't even hear you come in."

"I know, you were into that computer, and it almost made me a little jealous, the way your fingers were touching the keyboard," he whispered, kissing her by the side of her mouth. "Do you think I might get a chance to feel the same stroke of your fingers on my body?"

"It all depends if you were a good boy on your lunch break," she teased, standing up. "Did you do anything while I was out?"

"Anything...like what?" Richard asked, dodging her question.

She didn't miss the flash of apprehension that flashed in Richard's eyes before he answered her. What was he up to now? Did he go and see Emily after he said he wanted them to be a couple?

"Like you went to see Emily?" She didn't have time to be jerked around, not with Johnny on her back now for the money. "Hey...it's okay if you changed your mind about us." Dawn tried to move around Richard, but he blocked her path.

"I haven't seen Emily in days, and I have no need to see her. Why would I, when I have you in my life?" Richard asked, falling down into his chair and pulling her down with him. "I went to see Lee."

"Lee is very masculine, isn't he?"

"Are you saying that I'm not?" Richard asked by her ear, tugging her shirt from her skirt.

"You're sexy, and you know it."

"Sexy enough that you will be my date to a dinner party at Lee's house?" Richard unbuttoned her shirt and tossed it on his desk, leaving her only clad in a pink bra. "Does your underwear match this sexy bra?"

Dawn tried to keep a straight thought as her eyes met Richard's, but it was hard when such heat was pouring from him. "I can't tell you that. You shouldn't have taken my shirt off in the office. We can't be doing this here," she sighed, snatching her shirt off his desk and putting it back on.

"You're right. But when I see you looking so damn good, I can't help myself," Richard confessed, brushing his nose beneath her ear. "Will I get a chance to find out the answer to my question later?"

"Only if you promise to start working on that list I typed out tomorrow," she whispered, giving him a kiss.

Richard flipped her around so she was straddling his long legs. "Do you care about me as much as you do *D4?* I think you love this place more than you do me."

"No...that's not true. I do love...care about you," Dawn said, trying to correct her slip of tongue. "But you don't want to lose this restaurant, and I know that," she continued. "You hired me back to save this place, and that's what I'm going to do."

"Fine, but remember that your boyfriend needs a little TLC, too." After the words left Richard's mouth, his gaze raked across her face and then clung to her eyes, analyzing her reaction.

She tried to keep the startled look off her face, but she knew that she failed. "When did you become my boyfriend? We haven't even been out on our first date yet."

"First dates are for people trying to get to know each other. We are past that stage in our relationship. We are at the stage where all the kissing and hugging starts," he whispered, planting a kiss on mouth before she could stop him.

A delightful shiver of need raced through her as Richard ran his tongue along the side of her jaw and moved to nibble at the side of her neck. "Are you trying to seduce me, Mr. Drace?"

"First, I stopped being Mr. Drace months ago," Richard exclaimed, moving her back so he could stare into her eyes. "Secondly, hard as my cock is right now, the only thing I want you to call me is lover," he growled as he thrust his hips up to prove his point.

Gasping, she wrapped her hands around Richard's forearms and moved her body at the same tempo as his. "We can't do this," she moaned. She tried to stop the movement of her hips but couldn't.

"Why not?" Richard asked as he reopened her shirt and unhooked her bra's snap in the front. Dropping his head, he sucked at her hard nipple before drawing it into his warm mouth.

"Oh...that feels so good," she gasped, dropping her head down to his shoulder.

He let go of her nipple with a loud, wet pop. "Do you want to feel even better?" Richard muttered as his hands slowly pushed up her skirt, and he brushed his knuckles across her dampness. "Just say yes, and I can make that happen for you, Kitten." His long fingers traced the outside of her matching pink thong, making her want to agree to his suggestion.

Just as she was about to say yes, a soft voice interrupted her. "Richard, are you back there?"

Richard's hands tightened around her waist before he lifted her off his aroused body and quickly helped her back into her top. "Sorry...we'll finish this later," he promised in her ear. Turning her around, he gave her a small push towards the table and then took a seat behind his desk to cover up the huge erection he was sporting.

"Yes…I am," he yelled, staring at her across the room as she sat down at the table. "Come on back here…sweetheart."

Dawn's head whipped around at the endearment coming from Richard's lips. Who was he calling sweetheart after he just pulled her off his hard erection? She wanted to say something but decided to stay quiet. She wanted to see who was about ready to come through the door. Her mouth dropped at the sight of a very stunning and pregnant African-American woman walked through the door.

The woman glanced in her direction and smiled before she focused her eyes on Richard. She gave him a huge smile that made her gorgeous face even more beautiful than it already was.

"Richard…I thought you were going to meet me for lunch and help me pick out something for the baby's room." The woman laughed as Richard came around the desk and kissed her on the cheek.

Dawn held back tears as she started to gather up her things. Once again, Richard had made a fool out of her. When was she going to learn to stop jumping in head first with this guy? "I see that you're busy, so I'll come back later," she replied, heading for the door. She hadn't made it two steps before Richard had taken her stuff out of her arms and was dragging her over to the pregnant woman.

He wrapped his arm around her waist and hugged her to his side. She didn't miss how the other woman's eyes widened in shock before she schooled her features. "Dawn Summers, I would like you to meet my very pregnant sister-in-law, Traci Drace. She was the unlucky woman who married my brother Zack."

"Your sister-in-law?" she groaned, feeling stupid at her jealousy.

"Yes," Richard breathed by her ear, and then he turned his attention back on Traci. "Traci, this is Dawn Summers, my girlfriend and restaurant manager for *D4*."

"Nice to meet you," Traci said, smiling at her.

"You, too," Dawn said, still feeling a little embarrassed. She had to get away from Richard to sort out this sudden change in their relationship. "I really need to go," she said, removing Richard's hand from her waist. "I have a few things I want to check on before I head home."

Richard tilted her chin up with one finger and made her look at him. "Is everything okay?"

She almost melted at the concern in his voice. "Yes, everything is fine," Dawn answered, removing Richard's finger from her face. "I have an appointment with two salespeople about setting up some new advertisements for the restaurant."

"Can I see you later?"

Richard was really interested in them being a couple. She didn't know how to handle all of this. Was her dream really coming true after two years? "I should be home around six o'clock if you want to stop by. I could fix us something for dinner," she suggested.

"No, don't do that. You've had a long day. I'll bring something with me. All I want you to do is be ready with that gorgeous smile of yours." He smiled, giving her a quick kiss.

Dawn accepted Richard's kiss, and from the corner of her eyes, she noticed Traci sitting down with a huge smile on her face. She broke away from the kiss and nodded in her direction. "I really need to go. Have fun with your sister-in-law, and I'll see you later."

"You better believe that you will," Richard commented.

Walking back over to the table, she grabbed her stuff and strolled out the door feeling like a woman who almost had everything she needed in the world. Now the only thing she had to do was get that damn tape from Johnny, and her life would be perfect.

Chapter Fifteen

"Hello, Richard. Why haven't you called me lately?"

Richard placed the last of the grocery bags in the back of his vehicle and slammed the trunk shut. Of all the days, why did he have to run into Emily now? He only wanted to get a few things at the store and then leave to spend time with Dawn. This was going to be their first dinner tonight, and now because of Emily, he might end up running late.

"Emily, you know that I'm dating Dawn now," he sighed, turning to face the pushy twenty-something. He still didn't know why he got hooked up with her in the first place. "I thought I told you it was over between us weeks ago." He took a step back as Emily blew a puff of smoke in the air and glared at him.

"You dumped me on my answering machine while I was out of town visiting my sister," she spat, tossing her cigarette down on the ground between them. "What kind of guy does that to his girlfriend?" she asked, taking a step closer to him. "I thought we had something special between us." Emily wrapped her arms around his shoulders and brushed her body over his.

Removing her arms from around his neck, Richard shoved Emily away from him. He wasn't about to let her ruin what he was building with Dawn. No woman in the world made him feel the things that his alluring manager did. He had messed up once with Dawn, and he wasn't going down that same path again.

"You know we never had anything special, Emily, so why try to lie now and say that we did?" Richard sighed, walking around to the driver's side of his car. He unlocked the door and got in. He rolled down his window and waited for Emily to move so he could back out. "Why don't you do yourself a favor and find a nice guy closer to your own age?" he finished, pulling the rest of the way out and taking off in the direction of Dawn's house.

"No, I don't want a guy my age," Emily yelled at the back of Richard's car. "I want you, and I always get what I want."

* * * *

On the way to Dawn's house, Richard couldn't forget how Emily was looking at him as he glanced through the rearview mirror. She didn't look like a girl who was giving up without a fight. Dawn still wasn't quite sure about his feelings for her, and he couldn't have Emily putting any doubts in her head. Maybe he needed to make time to see her at the restaurant and make her understand that there wasn't anything between them. He was with Dawn now, and it was going to stay like that.

He hadn't realized how much he cared about Dawn until she was gone and he couldn't get her to come back. She was the part of his life that he had been missing, and he was going to do everything in his power to hold on to her. *D4* had been his entire life until Dawn knocked on his office door and walked inside.

The second he raised his eyes and stared into hers, he had wanted to know her better. Yet somehow things got turned around, and instead of pulling her towards him, he had shoved her away. Something he still regretted.

Richard wondered if he would be in a committed relationship now with Dawn, if he hadn't allowed his fears to take control of him. Back then, he wasn't strong even like Zack, and he wasn't ready to explore the passionate feelings he had for Dawn. However somehow fate had given him a second chance with the woman he loved, and he wasn't about to waste it. Dawn was his and always would be. Now he only had to make her believe it, which was going to be the hardest part.

* * * *

Dawn glanced at her watch and paced around the room while Johnny sat in one of her chairs and stared at her. "What are you doing here? Didn't I tell you that I don't have that kind of money?" Biting her lip, she wished that Johnny would leave before Richard showed up because she didn't have a clue how to explain why he was in her house.

"Aren't you going to give me a compliment on how nice I look?" Johnny asked, pointing to his new clothes and washed hair. "I saw how you turned up your nose at me at the restaurant."

She did wonder how Johnny got the new jeans, shoes, and t-shirt without having a job. "What did you do, rob some little old lady on the street for the money?" Dawn snapped, not caring about the tone of her voice. She needed Johnny out of her house ASAP.

"Don't get that tone with me, Miss Dawn Kristian Summers!" Johnny yelled back. "Or I might have to let Richard know what you were doing six months ago."

Dawn tasted bile as it rose up in her throat at the memory Johnny was bringing back to her. "You wouldn't dare do that to me. We have been friends way too long for that. Anyway, you want the money more than to expose the tape," she hedged, trying to see how far Johnny was willingly to go.

Standing up from the chair, Johnny came closer to her and circled her body. Reaching out, he ran his fingers across her lower back and leaned in to smell her hair. She tried not to flinch as the odor of his cheap cologne burned her nose. "The only way I'll let the money slide is if you go back home with me. You know that everyone thought we would be together forever."

Dawn stood perfectly still as Johnny brushed her hair to the side and ran his tongue across the back of her neck. She couldn't believe he thought she would want him after all the things he had done to get drugs. She couldn't let him have sex with her for anything in the world. "Stop it!" she hissed, jerking her body away from him. "I don't want your hands on me."

Cursing, Johnny wrapped his hand around her upper arm and hauled her body back against his. "That isn't what you said the night I had you in my parents' car behind the football field. You kept begging for me to keep making love to you over and over. Baby, you were a wildcat that night."

Dawn shook Johnny's hand off her arm and wiped off his touch. "That was years ago. I was young, and I didn't know any better." Eyeing him up and down, she wrapped her arms around her waist. She still couldn't believe she ever thought she was in love with this guy.

Smirking at her, Johnny fell back down in the chair and crossed his legs. "Here I thought that a girl never forgot her first," he taunted, winking at her. "I know that I remember those claw marks you left on my back. I never thought that would heal up, but I'm willing to give it another go if you are."

"I want you to get out of my house now," Dawn yelled. Running over to the door, she flung it open. "I don't want you to come back here again. If we need to talk, it will be anywhere but here. I can't afford to let Richard catch you here."

"Why can't you afford to let me find who's in your house?" a familiar voice whispered behind her.

Her body stiffened in shock as Richard brushed past her, carrying grocery bags in each hand. Bending down, he placed a kiss on her cheek while staring at Johnny, relaxed in her living room. "I didn't know you had company," Richard whispered. "Should I leave the two of you alone so you can talk?"

Closing the door quickly, Dawn moved to stand beside Richard, hoping against hope that Johnny wouldn't say anything to him. "Honey, those bags look really heavy. Why don't you go straight ahead and place them in the kitchen?" Placing her hand in the middle of Richard's back, she gave him a small shove. "I'll be there in a minute, after I show Johnny out."

Richard looked down at her, then back at Johnny before he took off in the direction of the kitchen. "Don't be too long. I don't want the food to get cold."

The second Richard's wide shoulders went into the kitchen, she raced over and jerked Johnny out of the chair and dragged him towards the door. "It's time for you to leave, and I don't want to hear another word from you," she hissed under her breath as she opened the door.

Shoving her uninvited guest outside, Dawn followed him out and closed the door behind them. "I don't want you to say a word to anyone about what you have," she said. "It's something that can be taken care of between the two of us."

"Well, you better find a way to earn some more money, or that tape will be all over the Internet in a matter of seconds," Johnny threatened. "I'm looking for a fix, so I don't have anything to lose. What do you think that guy in your kitchen would do if he found out about your video habits?"

The thought of Richard finding out what was on that tape tore at her insides as an icy fear twisted around her heart. "Richard isn't going to find out because I'm going to get your damn money." She glanced back at the door and then looked back at Johnny. "Just remember that after you have snorted it all up your nose; don't come back to me looking for more money."

Johnny's light brown eyes darkened to the point of almost being black. A long vein popped at the side of his head as he tried to control his quick temper. With difficulty, she managed not to flinch as he leaned closer to her. "Don't go there with me, Dawn. I still like you. That's why I haven't shown anyone else the tape, but if you keep pushing me, I'll do it."

"Sorry," she whispered, pressing her back into the front door. Her hand was itching so bad to slap the taste out of her former best friend's mouth, but she couldn't chance it with Richard inside.

"Good," Johnny smiled, showing a small gap between his two front teeth. "Now be a good girl and go inside to that new boyfriend of yours. He doesn't look like he likes to share." Tapping her on the cheek quickly, Johnny raced down the steps, got into his car, and drove off.

Dawn stood outside for a few more minutes after Johnny left, her mind working overtime in search of a way to explain him to Richard. She didn't know what she was going to say about him. "You don't have to explain yourself," she muttered. "Richard doesn't tell you about everything that goes on his life, and you don't need to tell him anything either."

The less he knew about Johnny, the better off he would be. Shaking the tension from her body, she turned the doorknob and went on into the house. "Hey, something sure smells good," she yelled, shutting the door behind her.

* * * *

"I think Dawn is seeing another man," Richard blurted out, joining his brothers at dinner table the next night. He had just come from working late at *D4* and needed someone to talk to about his problems.

"Why do you say that?" Zack asked, taking a sip of his lemon iced tea.

"I caught her with a man at her house yesterday," he answered, bringing his gaze over to his older brother.

"She was having sex with him?" Brad chimed in, shocked. "I didn't think she was like that. She came across as so sweet, almost innocent."

"I knew she wasn't as Pollyanna as she came across," Lee added.

`"No, she wasn't having sex with him, Brad," Richard bit out. "You shut up, Lee, because your hands are full enough trying to make Cherise not hate you."

"Then what did you catch her doing?" Zack asked, arching an eyebrow at him. "Were they playing strip poker or something?" he teased.

"If the three of you don't shut the hell up, I'm leaving and I won't be back," Richard threatened, giving all of his brothers the eye. "I came over here for help, not to get teased or taunted."

The room got very quiet as the other Drace brothers realized that Richard was serious. They were a little taken aback by the intense expression on their brother's face.

"I'm sorry; you're right. I shouldn't have said that about Dawn. I don't know her well enough to form that kind of opinion," Lee sighed. "I'm in a bad mood. Cherise is still fighting her feelings for me and it's driving me up the wall."

"I'm sorry, too, little brother," Zack's deep voice said. "I'm missing Traci because we had a fight a few days ago and she's staying at her sister's."

"I don't think I need to apologize for anything," Brad chimed in. "I just asked was she having sex. I didn't say that she was cheating on Richard."

Chuckling at Brad's comment, Richard waved off his other two brothers'apologies. "Don't worry about it. We're all under stress at the moment. I knew that none of you meant what you said about Dawn."

"So do you know who the guy was?" Lee asked.

Tapping his fingers against the table, Richard gave his head a quick shake. "See, that's the problem. Dawn went outside with this guy and then came back in like nothing ever happened. I don't know what I'm going to do about this."

He wanted to find out what Dawn was hiding from him because he knew it was something, but she wasn't about to tell him. Just as the tension between them was beginning to melt and he felt like that she might open up to him, this idiot came out of nowhere and was ruining everything. Was he the guy that she was always meeting for lunch? Or was he a past lover that was trying to get her back? From the looks of his long, stringy, blond hair, bloodshot eyes and five o'clock shadow, the guy in Dawn's house didn't look like someone she would want to share a bed with. Hell, he wasn't conceited, but he knew that he was a very good-looking man. He'd make sure that Dawn was in his bed before that other guy even thought up a plan to win his kitten over.

"Hey, what put that frown on your face?" Brad asked, waving his fork in the air.

"I was just thinking," Richard answered.

"About what?" Lee and Zack asked at the same time.

"Nothing that I need to tell you about now," he replied.

Chapter Sixteen

"We need to talk," Dawn said, brushing past him as she came into his house.

Richard closed his front door as he stared at the woman he had just fantasized about twenty minutes ago in his shower. His body was still humming from the orgasms that had shaken him; he was losing patience with holding back. He had wanted to give her time to get back into the flow of *D4*, but that cup was almost full. It was past time he got some of that attention.

"Good morning to you too, Kitten," he said, resting his back against the door. "To what do I owe the pleasure of my girlfriend visiting me this early in the morning?" Moving away from the door, he closed the distance between his body and Dawn's. He quickly jerked her into his arms and planted a kiss on her mouth. He didn't stop kissing her until she wrapped her arms around his neck and kissed him back.

"Now isn't this a much better way to greet your boyfriend instead of dishing out orders as soon as you see me?" he questioned by Dawn's ear as his fingers stroked her back.

"Sorry, all this being a couple stuff is still new to me. I promise I'll kiss you first next time, and then I'll bark out orders," Dawn teased, moving out of his arms. "But we really do need to talk," she stated, sitting down on the couch.

"Personal or business?" Richard questioned, joining Dawn on the couch. He wasn't about to let her end it between them. He wanted her in his life forever, and that was going to happen.

"For the moment, it's business," she said, turning to look him in the eyes. "We can get into the personal stuff later." Dawn pulled a sheet of paper from her pocket and handed it to him. "Read this and tell me what you think."

Taking the paper from her, he read over it and glanced back at her. "Do you think that this could really help us with the reopening of *D4?*" He wanted all the extra help that he could get, but he didn't like the idea of Dawn being gone.

"Are you sure that you're okay with me going to this?" Dawn asked. "I will be gone for at least three to four days. I want to mingle with other people and see what's *hot* out there right now in the restaurant world."

Richard tossed the sheet of paper on the table and pulled Dawn against his chest. "You're the best thing that has ever happened to me," he whispered by her ear, while his fingers pulled at the belt holding her dress together.

"You aren't bad yourself, Mr. Drace," Dawn sighed, resting her back against his bare chest. "I love working for you, and I'm going to keep my promise to you. I want you to have the restaurant the way you want it."

After getting the dress untied, he brushed it away from Dawn's body and ran his fingers across Dawn's stomach, smiling above her head when she jerked underneath his hand. "Can we spend some time together that you don't want to bring *D4* into the conversation?" he asked, sliding his fingers up to cup her breast through the purple bra. "I know we can find other ways to spend our time with each other."

"Do you want to play cards?' Dawn asked.

"No," he answered, unsnapping her bra.

"Scrabble?"

"Guess again," Richard whispered as he stroked her stiff nipples with his fingertips. Leaning back against the couch's arm, he pulled Dawn until she lay flat on his chest.

Dawn squirmed against him as his erection poked at her lower back. "Hangman?" She moaned as his other hand slid around her body and his fingers eased inside her underwear.

"Kitten, you're already so wet for me. Are you sure you don't want to be doing the same thing that I want to?" he asked, pushing two fingers easily inside her body. "How much longer can you wait? I want you so bad. I need to show you how much you mean to me."

Richard felt his cock thicken and harden even more when Dawn's muscle tightened around his fingers. "Baby, you're so tight. Has it been a while for you?" he questioned, licking his lips at the thought of being buried deep inside Dawn. "I swear I can make you glad that you haven't been with a man for a while."

Dawn shuddered as Richard's words washed over her body. "Are you sure that it's me that you want?" she asked. "Has it been a while since you've been with a woman?"

Withdrawing his fingers from her body, Richard flipped Dawn over so her breasts were pressed onto his chest. He groaned at how good their warm weight felt to him. How could she let the idea enter her mind that he wanted another woman's body in his bed? He wrapped his juice-covered finger under her chin and forced her to look at him.

"I don't know if I did something to make you this insecure about your sexiness and worth, but I'm going to everything I can to change it," he promised, placing a soft kiss on her mouth. "I only want you in my bed. I haven't been with any other woman since you left. I don't mind using a box full of condoms if that is what it will take."

Sliding his hands through her hair, he licked away the juices that lingered on her chin. "Dawn, you taste as warm and sweet as I knew you would." He cupped her butt and placed her directly over his erection. "What do you say? Can I cherish your body the way I've wanted to for the past month?"

Chapter Seventeen

Dawn's eyes smoldered as she gazed down into Richard's handsome face. His need was alive and glowing in his eyes while he stared up at her, waiting for a response. She had wanted this for so long that now that the time had come, she was more than a little nervous. Richard was right; it had been a while since she had been with a man. She could count her past lovers on one hand, but could the man with the corded body underneath her do the same thing?

"I want to say yes so bad, but I have to tell you something first," she answered. She couldn't make love to Richard until he knew about Johnny and the videotape. It would not be right to go down this road with that hanging over her head.

"Can it wait until after I get to make you mine?" Richard asked, slipping her dress off one shoulder. "I don't want anything to mess up this moment."

Richard was right. Why should she let Johnny take this away from her? She had been in love with Richard for so long; it was past time for this to happen between the two of them. Whatever happened afterwards, she would deal with later on.

"Yes. It can wait," she murmured, placing a kiss on Richard's firm mouth. "I want you. I've wanted you for a while," Dawn confessed.

"Kitten, I'm about to let you have all of me as many times as you want tonight," Richard promised, getting up from the couch with her in his arms. Carrying her across the floor, she guessed he was taking her in the direction of his bedroom.

"Richard, it's ten o'clock in the morning," she corrected as he kicked open the door to his bedroom.

"Yeah, and I plan on loving you all day long," he whispered as he stood her up in front of himself. Stripping the dress the rest of the way off her body, he tossed it into a chair next to the bed.

"You are so beautiful," Richard moaned, rubbing his hands across her breasts. "Do you know the first time I saw you, I envisioned what you would look like naked?" He kept moving closer, causing her to back up until the back of her legs hit the bed and she fell backwards. "I would wake up rock-hard at night after dreaming about taking you in my bed."

Dawn rose up on her elbows, clad only in a pair of bikini underwear, and ran her gaze over Richard. He stood there, devilishly handsome with his tempting, attractive male physique. He looked very sexy; his chest was wide, and his shoulders were muscular. Licking her lips, she reached out and tugged at the drawstring holding up Richard's sweatpants. "You're seeing everything I have to offer," she whispered. "Can't I see what I've been dreaming about, too?"

Brushing her hand away, Richard pulled at the string; his pants dropped around his feet, and he kicked them away. "I think you still have something on that you can take off," he whispered, waving a hand towards her underwear. "I don't want to be the only one here naked."

Dawn quickly took off her underwear and dropped them to the floor. She sat totally still as Richard's green eyes looked over her body. She wanted to cover up her breasts because they were the worst part of her body. They were way too large compared to the smaller parts of her. She raised her hand to cover herself when Richard wrapped his fingers around her wrist.

"What were you going to do?" he asked, placing her hand back down on the bed as he leaned over her body. His erection brushed the inside of her thigh, shooting electrical sparks through her entire system.

"I was going to cover up my breasts," she answered, staring into his eyes. "I've always hated how big they were. I might get a breast reduction in the next several months."

With a speed that she didn't know Richard had, he wrapped his hands around her shoulders and hauled her body against his. "I won't let anyone cut on this perfect body of yours. Your body was made for me, and my body was made for yours," he said, laying her back down on the bed.

"Why would you want to take away something as beautiful as these?" Richard asked, holding her breasts in the palms of his hands. "I could suck at them for hours and never get tired of loving them."

Opening his mouth, he twirled his tongue around her nipple and then sucked at it like it was a hard piece of candy. Moaning, she spread her legs open wider, and Richard settled between them, brushing the tip of his cock against her wet folds. Her body jerked at the first touch of Richard against her; he was so hot and hard, like a piece of steel.

Richard popped her nipple out of his mouth and then licked a trail from the valley between her breasts to her left ear. "Dawn, how much do you trust me?" his slightly accented, drawling voice asked.

"I trust you with everything that I have in me," she whispered, turning her head so she was making eye contact with the man she loved. Didn't Richard know by now that she would do anything for him?

"I want to do something with you, but if you get scared and tell me to stop, I will," Richard said, sliding off her. Reaching over, he opened the dresser by the side of his bed and grabbed a medium-sized black pouch.

Dawn eyed the velvet pouch in Richard's hand and wondered what he had in mind for her. She knew without a doubt how much he loved controlling every situation that he was in, but she wasn't too sure she wanted to participate in what he was thinking about now.

"What do you say?" he asked, rubbing the downy material across her breast. "I can promise it'll be an experience that you will never forget, Kitten."

* * * *

"If I say yes, will it make the sex hotter for you, too?" she asked, taking the pouch from his hand. "Then do you think I'll get the chance to do the same thing to you?"

Richard knew the last remaining amount of blood that he had left in his head filled his cock, making it even thicker, longer and harder for the

144

woman next to him. "Yes to both questions, my little kitten," he answered, taking the bag back from her. "It's all about trusting your partner. Do you trust me?"

A tense silence enveloped the room as he waited for Dawn to answer him. Out of all the things he had in his life, none of them compared to her reply. He needed for her to trust him with her body, because if she did then her heart wasn't far behind. His chest felt as if it would burst when Dawn glanced away from him at stared at the chair in the corner.

"Yes, I trust you, Richard, because I love you," she murmured, swinging her gaze back over to him. "I'm game to try what you have in mind as long as I can stop it any time I want to."

Richard felt a warm glow spread through him as Dawn's words washed over his body. *She loved him!* The woman he had chased away with his harsh words and tried to make jealous by shoving another woman under her nose loved him. He didn't know that three little words could make him feel so whole.

"Kitten, I love…"

"No…don't ruin our first time together by saying words you don't mean," Dawn pleaded, cutting him off. Linking her arms around his neck, she fell back on the bed taking him with her. "You have me wondering what's in that little pouch of yours."

Richard's eyes darkened dangerously, noticing the gleam of interest that came into Dawn's eyes. There was an invitation in those dark brown depths that she didn't know she was giving.

"How about you place your hands above your head and let me open it so you can find out?" he suggested, kissing the side of the mouth before he slid his body off hers.

Chapter Eighteen

Dawn raised her hands over her head and watched as Richard pulled a long black scarf from the pouch. He slipped it through his hands a couple of times as his gaze roamed all over her body. She felt like he knew her inner desires with the way he didn't leave a part untouched by his hot gaze. How had she lasted this long without giving in to her need to have this man inside her?

Richard was sexy as sin, and for the time being, he was all hers. She was going to enjoy him for as long as she could. Licking her lips, she watched as he leaned over her with the scarf in her hand. "What do you think you're going to do with that piece of silk?" Oh, she knew; she just wanted Richard to tell her. She had read books about men who enjoyed playing games during sex, but she never thought of Richard as one of them. She wondered what else her sexy man had hidden in his bag of tricks.

"I'm going to wrap it around your gorgeous wrists, then tie them to the bedpost," he answered as he worked the material around her wrists. Then he took the extra fabric and secured it around the post behind her head. "Are you comfortable?" Richard asked. "I won't get any pleasure from this if you're in pain."

She gave the scarf a couple of tugs and found that it was tight, but not uncomfortable. "No, it's fine." Dawn wondered if Richard knew how much courage this was taking on her part. She usually wasn't the kind of girl that let men tie her up to a bed.

"Are you ready for surprise number two?" Richard asked, brushing his palms over her nipples. "Do you know how beautiful you are? I could just look at you all night long."

"You aren't bad yourself," she answered, eyeing the erection that was poking at the inside of her thigh. How much longer did she have to wait to feel that piece of steel inside of her?

Leaning over, Richard traced the length of her stomach with his tongue, pausing a few seconds to dip it inside her navel and then nip at the flesh right below it. "You didn't answer my first question. Are you ready for your second surprise?"

"Yes."

"Good…because I couldn't wait much longer to give it to you." He stuck his hand inside the bag and pulled out a blindfold that matched the scarf tied around her wrists. "I want to blindfold you, Dawn. It's all part of the game, and I swear you'll love it," he promised as the words rushed from his mouth.

Taking a deep breath, she willed the last part of her nerves from her body; she didn't have time to be scared, when she knew deep down that Richard wouldn't do anything to hurt her.

"Go ahead," Dawn whispered. "I trust you with this, too." She saw the look of praise that came over

Richard's face at her eagerness, and she was pleased that she didn't let her uncertainty take over.

"Oh, Kitten, you don't know how much this means to me," Richard admitted as he leaned over and tied the blindfold lightly around her head. "What do you want your word to be?" he breathed by her ear as his tongue stroked the side of her ear.

She shivered at the unexpected sensation. It felt hotter since she didn't know it was going to happen. "Word?" Dawn gasped, swallowing down a moan.

"Yes, I need for you to give me a safe word so I'll know to stop if anything gets too hot for you," Richard replied by her ear. "I don't want to scare you away from a second time."

Dawn doubted that Richard could do anything to frighten her away from the moment. She had wanted him so badly these several months that anything he wanted to do with her would be appreciated to the fullest. But after thinking about it, she knew the perfect safe word.

"Chances," she answered, as Richard laid his body on top of hers and the hair from his chest tickled her breasts. As long as she lived, she knew there would never be a better feeling in the world.

"Chances?" he asked. "Why that word?"

"It's my middle name," Dawn joked, tugging at her wrists, pissed that she couldn't see the hot man above her or touch him. Maybe she shouldn't have agreed to this game after all.

The masculine chuckle coming from above her sent her nerve endings on edge. Richard was driving her wild with the cat-and-mouse game. She never knew when he was going to touch her. "Very unique, just like the appetizing woman beneath me," Richard mumbled.

She whispered, "Why aren't you touching me more?"

Dawn felt the bed dip as Richard rolled off her body. She sensed that he was standing next to the bed, but she couldn't be sure because he was no longer talking to her. Panic slowly started to set in at the thought of Richard leaving her alone, tied to his bed. "Richard, are you still there?" she asked, trying to hear any movement in the room, but the only thing she heard was silence.

"I'm right here, Kitten," Richard drawled beside the bed.

Why was he just standing there? Why wasn't he touching her? Was this part of the game?

"Why aren't you touching or kissing me?" she asked, turning her head in the direction she heard Richard's voice coming from. "Is there something wrong?"

"Yes, there is something wrong," Richard answered. The bed dipped as he sat back down. "Your body is so perfect I don't know where to start first," he praised, brushing the tips of his fingers across her stomach. "Should I start here first?" Richard asked, skimming his fingers against the underside of her breast.

Dawn jerked as a stream of heat shot between her legs. She tried twisting her body so Richard would touch the whole nipple, but he removed his hand from her breast completely.

Damn, she hated being tied up.

"Or should I go here instead? It seems to be calling me," Richard whispered as his knuckles suddenly brushed over her wetness. "I swear I hear something call me," he groaned. "Should I go investigate?" Richard asked as his fingers played with the curls between her legs.

Dawn was too turned on to speak, so she just nodded her head. She knew now why Richard wanted her tied up; so she would die before she got the orgasms that she needed. All of the quick brush here and another touch there wasn't giving her what she needed.

"I don't understand what you mean, Dawn," Richard exclaimed, pressing the palm of his hand against her. "I need to hear the words. Do you think you can give me those?"

"I want you to touch me," she moaned, lifting her hips. "Please."

"You don't have to beg," his silky voice whispered as two long fingers thrust into her body and a warm mouth wrapped around her nipple.

Placing her feet flat on the bed, Dawn raised her hips more so Richard's fingers went further into her body. She couldn't get over how deep his touch felt inside her. Was it because of the blindfold or because she had wanted this for so long? Whatever it was, she never wanted it to stop.

Chapter Nineteen

He studied the responsive woman beneath him as he sucked at her breasts, and everything he had wanted to experience with any other woman evaporated right out of his mind. Richard knew he was supposed to be at this place in his life. Dawn was supposed to wiggling her cute little ass under him as his fingers worked in and out of her snug body. He wanted to play this game with her to seduce her, but somehow she turned the tables on him, and he was the one getting seduced.

Richard had to find out how far he could go before Dawn's perfect well-placed control snapped. He didn't want his list-making, glasses-wearing restaurant manager in bed with him. He wanted the woman that he dreamt about in the shower in the morning, or the little sex kitten he craved to take him at work every day of the week. Restaurant Dawn was fine for D4, but here in his bedroom, he would get the woman he knew she could be.

Easing his mouth off her delicious breast, Richard sat back and continued to work his two fingers inside her body. He enjoyed how slick they were becoming with her essence. He slowly arched his hand and then inserted his first two fingers deeply until the pad of his thumb rested against her.

Richard twisted and wiggled his fingers inside Dawn until they became like a mini-vibrator.

Dawn started to pull at the sash holding her arms together. "Richard, you have to stop, you're killing me," she panted, arching her hips trying to match the movements of his fingers.

Moving his body gently over Dawn's, he used his free hand to massage her outer ear with slow, lingering strokes, giving it a playful tug here and there. "Do you like this? Does it make you want to explode all over my hand and the bed?" he groaned as he inhaled her aroma.

"You know it does," Dawn panted, still working her hips.

His cock was so painfully hard that he didn't think he could last a minute longer, but he had to until Dawn found her release first. All the other times he had been with a woman, it was for his need. However, this time he wanted to see Dawn's face when she found her climax. He wanted her face and the sound of her screams burned into his memory.

"Then, baby, come for me," he encouraged. "Let me see how beautiful you truly are. I'm so happy that you're my woman and I'm your man."

Dawn stopped moving her hips and clenched her muscles around his fingers. "I don't want you unless you are inside of me."

He knew what Dawn meant, but he wouldn't be able to last once he got inside her tight wetness. It would be his downfall and hers, too. This time was for her, and the next time would be for him. "No, I can't," he replied. "I want this time for you. I want to give you what you need. I can find my pleasure next time."

"No, I want you, not your fingers. I want...no, need to feel you deep in me," Dawn cried, twisting her head on the pillow. "Please. Don't you want to be inside of me, too? I know it will feel so good. I bet you're so hard and thick."

Hell, she sure knows how to make a man change his mind, Richard thought as he removed his fingers from Dawn's dripping body. He quickly removed the sash from her wrists and the blindfold from her head. She blinked at him a couple of times and then smiled.

"I liked that. I think we should do it again," she whispered.

Any other time, he would have loved hearing those words from Dawn's mouth, but his mind was only on getting inside her as quickly as possible. She wanted to know if he was hard and thick. Well, his little kitten was about to find out. He hoped that she was ready.

"Oh, we can try it again and other things, too," Richard whispered as he gently tugged Dawn until she was lying in the middle of the bed. "But right now, I want to be inside of you, and it can't wait." He took her legs and placed them on his shoulders, and he heard a small gasp come from Dawn.

"What are you doing?" she asked, resting her palms flat on the mattress. "Are you sure we can do it like this?"

Richard shook off the need to enter Dawn in one swift plunge and be buried balls-deep, but he almost lost control as the scent of her drifted up to his nose.

"You've never done it like this before?" God, he would love to be the first man to show her this position.

She shook her head as she made eye contact with him. "No, will it hurt?

Richard ran his tongue across his mouth as he thought of how good it was going to be for the both of them. He had only done this position one other time, and that woman was nowhere near as tight as Dawn. "No, Kitten, it won't hurt a bit. I promise it will leave you begging for more," he promised from his kneeling position in front of her as he thrust into her.

He bit back a curse as Dawn closed her eyes and purred in the back of her mouth. The warmth of her body fit his like a glove. Never had he been this deep inside a woman. Pulling out, he slid back in again and again, watching the play of emotions that crossed over Dawn's features.

Hot.

Warm.

Slick.

Home.

These were all the words that kept going through his mind as Dawn gasped and bucked under him. He loved the passion in her movements. It made her more womanly as he observed all of her last lingering insecurities crash around them.

"Is it good?" he asked, pulling out, sliding back in slowly to draw out Dawn's pleasure.

"Yes," Dawn panted, clawing at the bedspread under them. "Almost too damn good," she complained as her body writhed under his.

The sound of sweat-covered bodies coming together echoed in the room; it made him speed up the pace so the noise would rattle off the walls as the bed shook beneath them. Sweat dripped down the side of his face and down the rest of his body as Dawn held him tighter and tighter inside her. It almost seemed like he could feel her heart beating.

"It's better than good, Dawn," he groaned as he strained not to come until the amazing woman beneath him did. Taking his right hand away from her legs, he reached between them and stroked her until her screams rattled his eardrums. Placing his hand back on her thigh, he pulled out and thrust back in, finding his own shattering release a few seconds later.

Richard slowly eased out of Dawn's drained body and then rolled off the bed and lifted her off the bed into his arms. Tossing the sheets back, he gently laid her on the bed and joined her, covering them both with only a light green sheet.

"I'm never going to forget this night," she murmured, snuggling up against his chest as she drifted off to sleep.

"See, I told you it would be more than just good," he uttered, brushing a strand of hair away from her damp cheek. "It was the best day of my life because you trusted me, but more than that I learned that you love me, too," Richard whispered, staring down at the soft bundle in his arms. "You're mine now and forever. I'm going to marry you, and we're going to have a house full of kids." Kissing Dawn gently on the mouth so he wouldn't wake her,

Richard snuggled next to her and let the magic of the sandman carry him off to sleep.

* * * *

"Are you sure that you can't stay another day?" Richard questioned, wrapping his arms around the woman standing in front of him. "I thought we were having such a good time with each other." He didn't want Dawn to leave him at all. She had been staying with him since early Friday morning, and he loved waking up to her wrapped in his arms. He knew now what Zack felt when he first fell in love with Traci. He didn't want Dawn out of his sight for one second of the day.

"Yes, I can't keep wearing your t-shirt and shorts that are way too big, by the way," Dawn replied, running her fingers through the hair on his arms. "I need to get home and see if Hamilton Madsen called me."

White-hot jealousy shot through his entire body at the idea of Dawn waiting to get a phone call from another man. "Who in the hell is Hamilton Madsen, and why is he calling you?" he snapped, spinning Dawn around so he could stare into her eyes. He just had the best sex of his life and wanted to spend some time with the woman he was falling in love with, but she had plans with another man.

Dawn chuckled as she kissed him on the side of the mouth. "Hamilton Madsen is the liquor vendor. I set this appointment up two weeks ago. He suggested that we talk about it over a late breakfast," she sighed, pushing herself out of his arms. "I need to go home to shower and change clothes."

He still wasn't happy that his woman was having breakfast with a man whose name sounded like something out of an action movie. He sure in the hell better not resemble any famous Hollywood actors, and there was only one way to find out if Hamilton Madsen did. "Let me change clothes, and I'll go with you. He might have some questions for me," Richard said, heading towards the shower.

"No, you aren't going there acting like a jealous boyfriend," Dawn replied, stopping him in his tracks. "Have you finished contacting all those people on that list I gave to you? I really need feedback from them if we're going to have *D4* up and running."

Spinning around, he watched Dawn sit on the bed and slip her shoes back on. She had tried leaving yesterday while he was asleep. However, he had caught her at the door and brought her back upstairs and stripped her out of all of her clothes and then proceeded to show her why she needed to stay another night.

"I've heard back from four of them," he answered, bracing his shoulder against the bathroom door frame. "I left messages with the other ones."

"Why don't you call them while I'm with Hamilton and see can you get them?" Dawn said. Standing up, she pulled down her dress, covering up those toned legs he loved so much.

"Don't call him Hamilton," Richard said, "and don't wear a dress or a skirt. I don't want him looking at your legs."

Laughing, Dawn hurried around the bed over to him and wrapped her arms around his neck before kissing him on the mouth. Moving back, she gazed into his eyes. "Stop being jealous of a man you have never met, and please finish the list I gave you."

Sliding his hands down her back, he cupped her butt in his hands. "Wrap your legs around my waist," Richard said, staring at Dawn.

"We don't have time for this," she sighed as she wrapped her legs around him. "I'm going to be late for my meeting with Mr. Madsen."

He held her in place with one hand while the other one undid the buttons on her dress until her lacy bra showed. He undid the front snap with one tug, and one perfect brown breast popped out. Turning so that Dawn's back rested against the wall, he rubbed his fingers over her nipple until it hardened.

"God, I can't let you do this," she moaned as he pulled the tight bud into his mouth and sucked.

Richard sucked harder on Dawn's breast as he carried her back over to the rumpled bed and laid her back down. Removing her legs from his waist, he slipped his hand between her legs and gave her underwear a firm tug. They came away in his hand. He continued the sucking movement of his mouth as he thrust three fingers into her already damp body.

"YES," she screamed the second his fingers entered her body. He knew her orgasm was close, but he wanted her to work for it.

Richard slowly removed his mouth from the nipple that was giving him so much enjoyment to watch his woman struggle to find the release she needed. He slid his fingers as far into her as they could go and then he stopped. Dawn's eyes popped open. They were filled with an unfilled desire as she glared at him.

"What are you doing?" she asked as she wiggled her hips.

He placed his free hand in the middle of her stomach and held her still. "Who does this body belong to?"

Dawn narrowed her eyes at him. "Me."

He smirked at her spunk and then moved his fingers a little. She bit her bottom lip and closed her eyes as her hips tried to search for that release she wanted. "Wrong answer," he murmured. "Try again."

"I don't know," she lied.

He loved how Dawn was playing with him. He knew she needed this as much as he did, but she was still determined to fight it. Oh, he was going to love having her in his bed from now on. There wasn't ever going to be a dull moment; he could bet on that.

"Maybe I was wrong. I thought *my* kitten liked to be stroked," Richard sighed as he slowly eased his fingers out of Dawn's body, inch by inch.

"Your kitten does," she mumbled, opening her eyes as she reached down to grab his hand.

Smiling, he removed her hand, placing it at her side as he glanced back up and looked into her eyes. "Okay, last time for this question. Who does this tantalizing body belong to?"

"You…it belongs to you for as long as you want it," Dawn whispered, finally giving in and saying the words he wanted to hear.

"Good answer, Kitten," Richard agreed as he pushed his fingers back in her body and gave her the orgasm she craved. Seeing the sheer ecstasy on her face, he felt his cock jerk and spill his seed in the front of his pajama bottoms.

Chapter Twenty

"Mr. Madsen, I'm so sorry that I'm late," Dawn apologized, taking a seat at the table. "Something came up at the last minute, and I had to take care of it." She was so glad that Hamilton couldn't read minds, or he'd know what exactly came up and how Richard took care of that problem. She was going to kill Richard if they lost the liquor bid for *D4*. "I hope you haven't been waiting long."

"No, as a matter of fact. I just arrived here five minutes ago myself," Hamilton replied with a slight French accent. "I had to make a last-minute phone call back home to check on a family matter."

Dawn thanked her lucky stars for her good luck. Hamilton Madsen was one of the most renowned wine merchants in the country, and he had agreed to see her on very short notice. "Did you get all of the information that I faxed over to you last week?" she inquired, pulling another copy out from the stack of papers in her hand.

"Yes," Hamilton answered, "and I'm very impressed with the new direction you want to take *D4* in. I think I might be able to give you what you are looking for."

"Wonderful." She grinned, placing the report on the table. "Here's another printout with the qualities we might need to start out with," Dawn said, sliding the paper toward Hamilton across the table.

Picking up the sheet of paper, Hamilton skimmed it and then laid it back down. "I always like to check out the places I'm sending my wines to. Is there any way I can get a tour of D4 before I make my final decision?"

"I've another appointment today, so I wouldn't be able to do it," Dawn said, thinking about the lunch date she had an hour from now. "But I'm free all day tomorrow. I would be more than happy to show you around."

"Would that include another lunch date with you?" Hamilton flirted. "I always enjoy the company of a lovely woman."

Dawn tilted her head and grinned at Hamilton. She liked how he had his dark blondish-brown hair pulled back in a ponytail and the neatly trimmed beard covered his face, but Richard was the only man for her. Yet if she was still single and looking, Hamilton would definitely get a second look.

"I'm sorry, but I'm dating someone," she answered.

"Are you happy with him?" Hamilton asked, with a twinkle to his caramel-colored eyes. "Is there a small chance I could steal you away from him? I need a beautiful manager for my restaurant."

She couldn't believe she was getting a job offer while she was still working for Richard. What was Hamilton thinking? She couldn't give him an answer, not while she was still under contract to D4.

"You know that I can't give you an answer," Dawn laughed. "Why are you even asking me that anyway? I thought Shelby Betts was your manager at *Ultimate*." She shoved her other paperwork back into the stack and continued with her questions. "Plus I only want you to supply the liquor for us. Wouldn't the other thing be a competition between two rival restaurants?"

"I'm a business man, and when I see something good, I go after it," Hamilton stated. "Besides, the word around town is once *D4* is back up and running, you're leaving Richard anyway, so why shouldn't I get my offer in now?"

Dawn felt a sinking feeling in the middle of her chest. Hamilton was right. After everything was accomplished for *D4*, her time with Richard would be over. She hated to think about that, but she had to. Richard hadn't mentioned her staying any longer, so he must want her to keep their deal.

"How about I contact you after I'm done with *D4* and see if we can work something out?" she suggested. "I always heard good things about you."

"In or out of the restaurant?" Hamilton flirted with her. "I've been known to steam up more places than just my business."

"I'm talking about your business," Dawn murmured, trying not to notice the way Hamilton was ogling her.

Sensing that she was uncomfortable with the way the conversation was headed, Hamilton smiled at her and then leaned back in his seat. "Okay, I'm done flirting with you, Miss Summers. I can't promise I won't do it again, but for the rest of our meal, I want to know how I can help you."

Feeling more in her element now, Dawn reached inside her purse and pulled out her red notepad. "It would be wonderful if you could fax us a list of all of the different liquors you have," she stated, pleased with the change of subject.

* * * *

"You look awful happy this morning. Does a woman by the name of Dawn Summers have anything to do with that smile on your face?" Lee asked, sitting back in his leather chair. "I know how you were trying to get closer to her."

Richard flopped down in a chair, stretched his legs out in front of him and grinned at his older brother. He hadn't felt this contented in years, and Lee hit the nail on the head. Dawn had everything to do with it.

"I couldn't be happier," Richard agreed. "These last couple of days had to be the best of my life, and I hope that there are more in my future."

"Dawn finally gave in?"

He didn't want to tell Lee everything about his sex life, but he would let him on something. "Yeah, she finally gave in, and I hope it continues, because I love it and her."

His brother's eyes lit up with amusement as he leaned forward and rested his elbows on his desk. "What did Dawn say when you told her that you were in love with her? When is the wedding? She is going to stay now, isn't she?"

Richard didn't know how to handle all the rapid-fire questions that Lee was tossing his way. Everything was happening so fast, and he knew that Dawn loved him, but he didn't have a clue if she wanted to get married. Hell, he wasn't positive that he wanted to take that walk down the aisle anytime soon.

"I don't know if Dawn is thinking about walking down the aisle with me or not," Richard said. "We really just started dating each other. We shouldn't jump ahead of ourselves too soon."

"Are you telling me that Dawn finally had sex with you, but you don't think that means she's thinking about the white picket fence and all the trimmings?" Lee questioned, moving back in his seat. "Don't you want to have kids with her?"

He would love to start a family with Dawn, but the marriage thing did scare him a little. What if he wasn't cut out to be a husband? Dawn liked her space sometimes, and half the time, he wanted to know where she was every second of the day. A marriage shouldn't start out like that.

Dawn was such an independent woman when she wanted to be, and that worried him. He was used to females wanting him around them all the time, like Emily. Could he let up some of his possessive ways and let Dawn breathe when she needed to?

"I don't know if I could be a good husband like Zack. Look at how he does everything for Traci, now that she's pregnant."

Lee chuckled. "Why are you sitting there lying? You know Zack did everything for Traci before she got pregnant. It got worse after they found out about the baby."

"Did he tell you that Traci's having a boy?" Richard asked.

"You know he called me right after he called you," Lee stated. "I'm still surprised that Zack was the first one of us to get married."

"Not any more than I was," Richard added, "but I think he had liked Traci for a while and never knew how to approach her."

Lee nodded in agreement. "It is hard when you like someone and you don't know what their feelings are for you."

Richard knew Lee wasn't talking about Zack anyone. The last time he talked to Zack, he told him that their feisty sister-in-law Cherise wasn't giving Lee the time of day. "Cherise still giving you the runaround?"

Lee gave his head a small shake and then sighed. "See, that's the problem. Cherise avoids me. I was over at Zack's yesterday, and she was there. She didn't stay ten minutes after I walked in the room."

He felt bad for Lee. Cherise didn't have to treat his brother like that. Lee was a handsome guy, and a lot of women would love to spend time with him. "Why don't you forget about her and move on?"

"Can you move on from Dawn if she decides to leave after D4 is taken care of?" Lee tossed back. "It's hard to let go of a woman when you know she's the one."

Richard instantly regretted his words. Lee had been in love with Cherise since the second he laid eyes on her, but she still blamed his brother for taking her antique show away from her. "Do you think she'll ever forgive you about her shop?" he asked. "I don't understand how she forgave Zack, but you're still on her most hated list."

"I think it's more than that," Lee uttered. "I believe Cherise is scared that she could fall in love with me."

"What? A controlling, overbearing, know-it-all?" he teased.

"No, a white man," Lee murmured.

Richard was shocked to hear that Cherise still had those views. She had seemed okay at her sister's wedding. What happened to change her mind? "She doesn't want to date you because you're white, and that's the only reason?" he questioned, amazed.

Shrugging his shoulders, Lee glanced away from him. "That seems to be the only reason she keeps turning me down."

Richard rested his elbows on his knees and leaned forward. "Hey, look at me." He waited until he had his brother's undivided attention. "If you really want Cherise, go after her. Don't let anything stand in your way. Prove how wrong she is."

"I thought you weren't fond of our outspoken sister-in-law's sister," Lee solicited.

"She's all right for you, but a little too untamed for me."

"Untamed?" Lee laughed. "Cherise would kill you if she heard that word come out of your mouth."

"Are you going to tell her?" Richard asked, sitting up in his seat. "I don't want her mad at me."

"No, I won't say a word to her," Lee replied." So, why don't you tell me where Dawn is?"

The name Hamilton Madsen flashed across Richard's mind, and he didn't like it at all. "She's at a late breakfast with a liquor vendor named Hamilton Madsen."

"You let her go out to lunch with Hamilton Madsen?" Lee exclaimed, a hint of surprise in his voice.

"What? Why should I not let Dawn meet with him?"

"All the rumors I heard about him over the years said that he's a real ladies' man. And that every woman he meets with ends up in his bed sooner or later. Hey, where are you going?" Lee yelled at Richard as he jumped up from the chair and headed for the door.

"I'm going to find Dawn and make sure she doesn't get added to that list," Richard said.

Chapter Twenty-One

Dawn gathered her paperwork together as Hamilton stood up from the table. "Are you sure that I can't talk you into having dinner with me tonight? Or even better, maybe breakfast in bed?"

She slid the rest of her paper into her attaché case and sat it back on the floor by her chair. She had to give Hamilton credit; he was a man who went after what he wanted, but in her heart, she already belonged to another man. "I'm sorry. I have to say no to both, but I wouldn't mind if you walked me out to my car," she suggested, standing up from the table.

Hamilton smiled at her, adding a twinkle to his chocolate eyes. "I love any time I get to spend with a gorgeous woman, so I'll be more than happy to escort you to your car." He waited while she finished getting her purse off the chair and picked up her case.

"You are just too cute for your own good," she teased Hamilton as he strolled beside her out the door. "You're going to make it so hard for a woman to win your heart."

"I'm not planning on walking down the aisle anytime soon, Miss Summers. Unless you're proposing to me. Then I might have to say yes," Hamilton teased, winking at her.

Dawn stopped at her car, unlocked it and tossed her stuff into the back seat. "I don't think we'll last past two weeks. You're too much for me," she commented, turning around to face Hamilton. "Besides, I don't think I could be married to you and work for Richard all at the same time."

"See? Another good reason to leave Drace and come to work for me," Hamilton stated. "I'll be the perfect boss, husband and lover," he grinned, wiggling his eyebrows as a smile spread across his tanned face.

She looked at Hamilton with amused wonder. Out of all the vendors she had met within the past three weeks, he was the funniest. She still couldn't get over how he was flirting with her. "Sorry, I can't do that. A promise is a promise," Dawn sighed, getting into her car. "I have to stay with Richard until D4 is back up and running."

Hamilton reached inside his suit jacket and tossed a card into her lap through the open window. "When your time is up with Richard or you just get bored to death of that drawl of his, call me and I'll find a place for you under me...I mean, with me at my restaurant," he corrected with a wink.

Picking up the card, she laid it on her dashboard, feeling a little special at the attention Hamilton was showering on her. It was nice to have an attractive man flirt with her, but her heart was with Richard. "You shouldn't give a poor girl like me ideas," she teased back. "I might just show up on your step one day begging to be with you...at your restaurant," she added.

Hamilton leaned into the car and ran his finger down the side of her face. "I just love it when a woman can flirt back with me. You're very tempting, Miss Summers, but I know you belong to Drace. I just hope he knows what a lucky man he is," he mumbled as he moved back from her car and turned back towards the restaurant.

"I hope he does, too," she answered as she watched Hamilton saunter away from her.

* * * *

"God, I thought didn't think he would ever leave," a voice snapped as her passenger door slammed shut.

Dawn spun around in her seat and gasped as she stared at Johnny, sitting in the seat next to her. "What in the hell are you doing here?" she hissed. "Have you been following me?"

"Damn skippy. I have been following your cute little ass," Johnny muttered, picking up Hamilton's card. "Hey, he really seemed into you. Do you think he'll give you the money I want?" he asked, shoving the card into his jeans. "Maybe I need to have a meeting with him and find out."

Dawn leaned across the seat and dug the card out of Johnny's pocket, shoving it into her purse. "Don't you dare go asking him for money or anything else, you bastard," she snapped. "I told you that I'll get you some money, but not the amount you want. You know that's way too much."

Johnny moved the seat back and propped his feet up on her dashboard before folding his arms behind his head. "I thought this Richard guy was rolling in money. I know that Lee has his own marketing business; Zack is a real estate developer with a very sexy pregnant wife, by the way; and Brad is a tennis instructor, and he also works for Lee."

She choked down the fear building up in her mouth, and then a shiver of panic hit her. "How do you know about Richard's family?"

"You'll be surprised at the things you can find out around here when you ask the right people," Johnny exclaimed.

"Who have you been talking to?"

Johnny dropped his feet off the dashboard and sat back, smirking at her. "I can't tell you all my secrets now, can I, Dawny?"

"Don't call me that," she snapped.

"You loved it when I called you that years ago," Johnny murmured as he ran his hand up her thigh. "Do you remember when I would call you that?"

Dawn slapped Johnny's hand away from her body and rested her back against the driver's side door. She wanted as much space between them as possible. "How many times to do I have to tell you that was the past and leave it there?"

"Sometimes it isn't a bad thing when you relive the past, Dawny," Johnny whispered, licking his lips. "I know that I still want you now, more than I did back then. You have filled out quite nicely from the girl I slept with back in high school," he said in a nasty tone as his gaze dropped down to her breasts.

Shivering from the heated, lecherous stare, Dawn tried to wrap her arms around her chest, but Johnny grabbed one of her hands and shoved it between his legs, making her cup an erection. "See, he still remembers how good it felt to be in your

173

moist warmth. Are you sure you don't want to visit that place again?" Johnny asked as he bucked his hips against her hand.

"You bastard," Dawn yelled as she snatched her hand back and wiped it down the front of her skirt. "Get out of my car now!" she screamed, shoving Johnny in the shoulder. Just thinking about having Johnny inside her again shattered the small ounce of control she was trying to retain. "I don't want you, and it's best that you stay away from me before I call the cops," she threatened.

Johnny laughed at her as he got out of the car and slammed the door shut. "Don't make threats you aren't going to keep, my little dawn flower, because I don't have anything to lose, but you have so much more."

"I'm not kidding, Johnny," Dawn tossed out her window as she started her car. "Stop following me, and leave me alone," she yelled as she drove off, leaving Johnny laughing at her in the distance.

* * * *

"Will you go to dinner with me tomorrow night at my brother Lee's house?" Brad asked the adorable woman standing in front of him, wiping sweat off her neck. He liked how the baby blue tennis outfit brought out Alicia's perfect toffee coloring.

"I don't know if I can, Brad," Alicia said, dropping her towel down on the bench. "You know that I have to get up early for the news report Thursday."

Brad hated how Alicia always talked to him like he was a buddy instead of a grown man who was in love with her. He had tried everything under the sun to get her to notice him as more than just a friend, but she wouldn't do it.

"Why are you turning me down? Didn't you go to that Halloween party with me last year?" he questioned. "What's so different about having dinner at my brother's? It will just be a little get together."

Alicia smiled at him as she pulled him down to sat beside her on the bench. "I went to that party with you as a friend, but this dinner is totally different. Does your brother think I'm your girlfriend?"

"No, Lee and my family think I'm bringing a good friend over for dinner," Brad lied. He wasn't about to let Alicia know that he was slowly moving towards that with their relationship.

"If it's just that, then I guess it wouldn't hurt if I had dinner with your family," Alicia agreed. "Anyway, Max will be out of town on business, so he won't miss me anyway."

He felt a knife go through his heart. Alicia had such a crush on her neighbor, but when would she realize that Max didn't see her in the same light as he did? Max never paid attention to her unless he wanted something, and Alicia always jumped when he called. If he had anything to say about it, that was going to stop. "How long will Max be gone this time?"

"I think for almost a year. He's doing a lot of stuff overseas for a special piece that is supposed to air then," Alicia said. "I hope I can find something to do to keep my mind off of him."

I can think of a lot of things for you to do, Brad thought. "You're welcome to hang out with me as much as you want," he suggested.

"You're so sweet," Alicia murmured, leaning over to kiss him on the cheek, but he moved his head so her mouth landed on his instead. The kiss only lasted a few seconds, but it was the best kiss of his thirty years. Alicia's lips tasted so full and plump against his. He wanted the kiss to go on forever, but Alicia broke it and moved back from him.

"What was that?" she whispered, running her tongue across her bottom lip.

"I don't know," he lied. "Why don't we try it again?" he suggested, easing closer to her until he heard his name being yelled in the background. Cursing, he glared over his shoulder at Richard hurrying towards them. "Great," Brad muttered under his breath.

"Who's that?" Alicia asked.

"My brother Richard," he answered, spinning around to look back at Alicia and frowning when he saw her gathering up her things. "You don't have to leave. Maybe we can do something after he leaves."

"No, I need to go home," Alicia said, jumping up from the bench and then grabbing her bag. "I'll call you later and finalize our dinner plans," she said, before she darted away through the gate that his brother was walking through.

"Has anyone told you that you have the world's worst timing?" Brad snapped at Richard as soon as he was within earshot.

Richard totally ignored his outburst as he joined him on the bench. "Wasn't that Alicia that just ran past me like the hounds of hell were after her?"

"Yeah, I was talking to her until you ruined it by showing up," he muttered at his brother.

"Sure, you were only talking," Richard laughed. "By the way, that's a nice shade of lipstick on your mouth."

Brad quickly wiped his mouth with the back of his hand. "Are you here to pick on me, or did you come for a reason?"

"I came here for a reason. I wanted to make sure that you kept up your end of the plan about Dawn," Richard stated. "You can start following her tomorrow during her lunch break."

He still couldn't believe that Richard wanted him to spy on Dawn like this. His brother had to know that this wasn't going to turn out well in the end. "I'm not so sure if this is still a good idea. I know that the two of you are getting closer. Why don't you ask Dawn where she's going every day for lunch?"

"Don't you think I have asked her already?" Richard questioned. "She is very tight-lipped about it."

"I suggest that you try again."

"No, this is the only way I know I'll be getting the truth," Richard exclaimed. "Dawn is so secretive sometimes, and if there's something going on with her, I want to know about it."

"Do you think it might have something to do with D4?"

Richard sighed. "I honestly don't know, but I want to find out. Dawn still doesn't understand that I'm here for her and will help her any way that I can."

"Have you ever given her a reason to feel she can come to you with her problems? As I recall, the last couple of times she did, you jumped on her and took the other person's side," Brad informed Richard.

"I hope her opinion of me has changed since we slept together," Richard blurted out.

Brad's blue eyes almost popped out of his head at that news. His brother had finally seduced the sexy Dawn into his bed. He wondered why it had taken him this long to make it happen. "I'm guessing this means things are over between you and Emily?"

He moved back before Richard's fist connected with his face. "Hell...yes, it means that I'm done dating Emily. What kind of guy do you think I am anyway?"

He answered his brother's question the only way that he knew how: honestly. "You've always put the two of them against each other in the past. How did I know this would be any different? Does Dawn know this is the real thing, or is she thinking you're only sleeping with her until she leaves D4?"

"Dawn isn't going to leave me," Richard responded.

"Are you sure about that?"

"Yes, I'm sure, and once you find out where she is going during her lunch break, I won't have to worry that about that anymore. Everything will be perfect."

"I hope you know what you're doing," Brad sighed.

"I do," Richard countered.

Chapter Twenty-Two

"Are you having a good time?"

Dawn rested her back against Richard's chest as he wrapped his arms around her waist. They stared out at all the trees surrounding Lee's house. It was a warm June night, and everything was perfect. She couldn't believe how well the dinner party went.

"Yes, I'm having a really good time," she answered, placing her hands on top of his. "I'm surprised how nice Lee treated me. From the stories I heard, he can be a real pain in the ass when he wants to be."

She felt Richard's chuckle at the back of her neck. "Lee does have a hard-handed way of dealing with people sometimes, but he has mellowed out a lot lately."

"Does it have anything to do with Cherise?"

"What makes you say that?"

"You had to notice the way his eyes never left her all through dinner. I thought he was going to get up and follow her when she got that cell phone call," she exclaimed, remembering the look on Lee's face.

"Lee is very fond of our sister-in-law's sister," Richard replied.

"Your brother is crazy about Cherise, so why aren't they a couple?" Dawn asked.

She moaned when a pair of firm lips brushed against the back of her neck. "I don't want to spend this time talking about my brother or Cherise," Richard growled. "I want to know if you're going to stay with me tonight."

Dawn felt a hedge of disappointment that Richard didn't want more than that from her. She loved making love to him, but she wanted to be more than a warm body in his bed. She had dreamt of a whole future with the attractive man behind her. However, he still only saw her as a means to an end, with benefits. "Ummm...I don't think that would be a good idea," she murmured, moving out of his arms. "I have another early morning appointment tomorrow, and I can't be late for it."

Richard reached for her, but she brushed off his hand. "Dawn, what's wrong?"

"Nothing," she lied, turning around to face him. "Why don't you tell me what the deal is with Brad and Alicia?"

"Brad is in love with her, and she only thinks of him as a friend, end of story. Now are you going to tell me what's wrong with you?" Richard said, reaching for her again and tugging her to his body. "You have been really quiet all through dinner, and then you came over here, away from the others."

Dawn shook off her dreams of having a life with the man in front of her and kissed him on the mouth. "Richard, I'm fine. I only wanted a little time to myself. How about we got back and join the others by the pool?"

Richard let her drag him back over to the pool where his family was, but she knew this conversation was far from being over. She didn't want to take tonight and discuss what the future might hold for them because she already knew. She'd rather watch the other couples interact with each other instead of dealing with her problems with Richard and his lack of feelings for her.

Walking back over to the patio table, she took a seat next to Cherise and smiled at Traci and Alicia, while Richard went back into the house to find Lee and his brothers.

"So you're the famous Dawn that Richard is always talking about," Cherise stated with her uniquely colored eyes staring straight at her.

"I don't think I'm as famous as you," Dawn tossed back. "Richard's always talking about how you keep his brother Lee on his toes," she exclaimed. "Lee doesn't seem all that bad, so why aren't you giving him a chance?"

"You know nothing about my relationship with Lee," Cherise said.

"The way I hear it, Lee is in love with you, but you won't give him the time of day," Dawn commented, watching the older woman fidget in her seat.

"Where do you get your information?" Cherise asked.

"I listen when people talk to me," Dawn replied.

"You need to stop listening to those people," Cherise said. "Gossip is the worst thing to listen to."

"Cherise, be nice to Dawn. She's only stating the truth," Traci chimed in, rubbing her swollen stomach. "Lee does have feelings for you, and you know it."

Dawn couldn't hold back the smile that covered her face as Cherise glared at her sister. "You keep quiet."

"You're just mad because you know I'm right," Traci grinned at her sister and then winked at her.

Right at that moment, Dawn felt like she belonged with Richard's family, and she was really going to miss this when she left to find another job and leave him in her past. It didn't matter where she went to work; Richard would always have a section of her heart. Pushing her sorrow to the side, she directed her attention to Alicia, who hadn't said much since she sat down at the table.

"What about you? Is there a future with you and Brad?" she inquired.

"Now if I'm in denial about my feelings for Lee, then Ms.Hart wrote the book on it," Cherise cut in.

She laughed as Alicia's mouth fell open at Cherise's comment and then joined in with the laughter as Traci teased her sister for the second time that night. Yeah…she sure was going to miss this in a few months.

Chapter Twenty-Three

"Why are we hiding out in here instead of going out there with the women we love?" Richard asked, resting his back on the breakfast bar watching his brother's move around the kitchen.

"I'm in here because Traci is still a little pissed at me," Zack said, placing his empty glass inside the dishwasher.

"Are the two of you still fighting this close to her due date?" Lee asked, popping a chip into his mouth from the bowl in the middle of the table. "I thought the two of you were joined at the hip."

"We were until I told her she needed to stay at home with the baby and let me be the one who worked," Zack replied, slamming the dishwasher shut. He flipped the on switch. "She didn't like that too much."

"In so many words, you told her that her place was at home while you earned all the money?" Brad butted in. "No wonder Traci's upset with you. She doesn't look like the kind of woman that wants to stay home, barefoot and pregnant. Besides, isn't she about ready to graduate from college?"

"I don't think Zack meant like it that," Richard cut in, trying to defuse a bad situation before it got started. "He only wanted Traci to take some time off before she went back to work."

Zack looked at Richard before he cut his eyes over to Brad, who was standing next to Lee at the table. "It was good that you jumped in there and helped Brad out because I was about to tell him to go to hell after a comment like that."

"Guys, let's not argue when we have four gorgeous women out there waiting for us," Lee said, heading for the door.

"I didn't know that Cherise was waiting for you, Lee," Richard teased, following Lee toward the patio doors.

"Neither did I," Zack and Brad cut in, going in the same direction as their brothers.

"She is. Only she doesn't know it yet," Lee tossed back over his shoulder.

Richard chuckled at Lee's confidence at how easily he thought he was going to win Cherise over. His brother had better wake up soon, because their outspoken sister-in-law's sister didn't look like she was looking for a husband anytime soon.

* * * *

"Hey, it looks like we lost a person," Richard said, taking a seat beside Dawn at the patio table. "Who ran Cherise off?" He wondered if anyone else saw the look of disappointment that passed over Lee's face when he noticed Cherise's empty seat.

"She got a phone call from David. He needed her help, so she left about five minutes ago," Traci said.

"Who's David?" Richard asked because he knew that Lee wasn't about to.

"A guy that she works with her at the marketing firm. They have become really close over the last few weeks," Traci said. "I think she even catered a party for him and his wife last week."

Wrapping his arm around the back of Dawn's chair, Richard kissed the side of her mouth. He was rewarded with a huge smile while he enjoyed the sounds of the crickets and birds. The thing he loved about his brother's house was the way it could relax the stress from his body.

"Lee, are you still planning to do some freelance work after you finish up that project at work?" he asked.

"Yes," Lee responded, glancing away from Cherise's empty seat. "I'd already decided on the business back when Zack and Traci got married. The man over the company had just gotten out of the hospital, so I'm giving him a few weeks to recover before I show up."

"Why are you freelancing away when you already have your own company?" Brad asked.

"I missed the rush of starting at the bottom and working your way up," Lee replied with a faraway look in his eyes. "Besides, I know you can handle the business without getting distracted while I'm gone."

Richard hurried up and jumped in before Brad got himself into another argument with one of them over something silly. "We have all the confidence in the world that Brad will do a good job," he stated, ending any response that Brad might want to come back with. From the corner of his eye, he noticed that Dawn was getting restless in her chair. He forgot that she was used to all of the verbal back-and-forth between him and his brothers.

"Guys, I hate to leave you, but I need to take Dawn home. We have a lot to get done tomorrow, and I don't want her falling asleep on the job," he teased, smiling down at Dawn as he got up and helped her out of her seat.

Richard stood to the side and let Dawn tell everyone at the table goodbye before he led her away to his car. He already knew the answer to his question, but he decided to ask it anyway. "Do you want to spend the night at my house? We can drop by your house, pick up some clothes and drive to work from my house in the morning." He got in on his side and started the car.

"That sounds wonderful," Dawn replied, surprising him, "but I'm not up for anything else tonight."

He would take what he could get, and if that was waking up with Dawn wrapped in his arms, he would take it. "Kitten, I don't have to make love to you every time we go to bed. Don't get me wrong; I love when we are together like that. But if you can't get any pleasure from it, neither can I," Richard said, letting go of the wheel to place his hand on her leg.

"Thanks for understanding," Dawn whispered, laying her head on his shoulder.

"Is there something you aren't telling me?" Richard asked, noticing that Dawn hadn't been full of her usual spunk.

"No, I'm fine," she answered, lifting her head to look at him. "I only need to crash in the bed in your arms, and I'll be a lot better," Dawn said, moving away from him to rest her head on the passenger seat.

Richard didn't believe what Dawn was telling him, but he didn't have time to go into it tonight. However, he would get to the bottom of what Dawn was keeping from him. He would bet that it had something to do with all the lunches she kept having away from the office. He would make sure that Brad reported back to him as soon as he found anything out. Dawn was his everything now, and he wasn't about to lose her.

"It looks like my sleeping beauty needed her sleep," Richard muttered, glancing over at Dawn, who was sound asleep. "And I'm going to do everything in my power to be the Prince Charming that she needs."

* * * *

The next morning, Dawn relaxed at Richard's desk and checked her emails while he made coffee in the kitchen. He was even sweet enough to buy her some banana nut muffins before he came to the restaurant. She couldn't get over how she woke up to him playing with her hair and kissing the side of her face. She never envisioned Richard as the cuddly type. He came across as too strong for that, but she wasn't going to complain. She kind of liked the softer side he showed in the bedroom. Scrolling down the page, she noticed Hamilton Madsen's email address and clicked on it to see what he had sent to her.

Hey gorgeous,
Have you decided to leave Richard and come to work for me yet? The offer is still open and available. I might

even be swayed to give you a raise after a kiss or two. Okay, all kidding aside. I've attached the wines I have to offer plus the other liquor selections I'm getting involved in. Look over them and call me; we can schedule another 'romantic' get together.

Hamilton.

Laughing at the email, Dawn moved her mouse over to the attachment and clicked on it twice to pull it up. She was really impressed with how quickly Hamilton got back to her with the information that she wanted. He might end up being the best investor she could have chosen to help *D4*. After a second or two, the attachment finally appeared in front of her.

Wine List
2005 Believe Magum
2005 Boyd Cantenac
2005 Clos St. Martin
1996 La Lagune Nicolas (Red)
1996 Cos D' Estrournel (Red)
1970 Durcu (Red)
1966 Pommard Clos Micto (Red)

Vodka
Vanilla
Raspberry
Ursus Rotter (has a fruity spicy taste)
Stolichanya
Stoli Persik – (has a sweet ripe peach taste)

Whiskey
Kentucky Straight Bourbon Whiskey

Old Island Single Malt Scotch Whiskey
Old Special Reserve Straight Bourbon Whiskey
Old Family Reserve Kentucky Straight Whiskey

Champagne
Georges Vesserre 1999 Grandgu
Georges NV Grand Cro Brut
Charles Heidsiek 1985 "Charlie"
Polroger 1996 Brut

Beer
Anchor Brewing
North Coast Brewing Co. Anniversary Kale
George Gale & Co. Prize Old Ale.
Unirbrove La Fin Du Monde

Printing out the in-depth list, Dawn picked up the phone and dialed Hamilton's number. She couldn't just send him an email after all the time he took getting this list together for her. She knew that there were a lot of liquors available, but she never had a clue so many varieties were out there. The phone rang a couple of times before Hamilton answered with his sexy accent.

"Hamilton Madsen," the rich voice answered over the phone.

"Hamilton, I had to call and thank you for the list that you emailed over. I had no clue that you had so many different brands," she answered, scanning the list and marking off the ones she thought Richard needed to try.

"I'm a man of many talents, and I would love a chance to prove it to you," Hamilton flirted.

"Didn't we already go over this?" Dawn questioned. "I thought I told you that I don't date men I work with."

"Technically, you don't work for me. I work for you, so what's the problem?" Hamilton shot back.

She held back a laugh at how clever Hamilton was at tossing her own words back at her. "You know that I can't do that."

"Is it because of Richard?" Hamilton murmured. "I didn't see a ring on your finger. It must not be that serious, so why can't I get one little date?"

"We have a date two days from now," Dawn replied, remembering the late lunch they had scheduled to finalize the liquor choices.

"You know that isn't the kind of date I was talking about, but hell, I'll take what I can get and pray Richard will screw up," Hamilton exclaimed. "I need to go because I have a meeting in twenty minutes. If you want any samples of the items on the list, let me know, and I'll send them over to D4."

Dawn was taken aback by how nice Hamilton was being to her. If she wasn't already in love with Richard, Hamilton might have gotten more than a passing glance from her. "Thanks so much for the offer. I might take you up on that," she replied. "Have a nice meeting."

"No. Thank you. Hearing your sweet voice has made my day," Hamilton whispered before he hung up the phone.

Not realizing that a smile covered her face, Dawn hung up the phone and had started to glance over the liquor list again when an infuriated voice snapped from the doorway. "What offer is Hamilton

Madsen giving you, and are you going to take it?"
Richard retorted.

Chapter Twenty-Four

Great! Out of all the times he could decide to walk in, it had to be now, Dawn thought as she raised her eyes to find Richard standing in the doorway, holding two cups of steaming coffee.

"It's nothing to worry about," she commented, getting out of her chair. Walking over to Richard, she took her cup of coffee out of his hand and kissed him on the cheek. "You're such a sweetheart to bring breakfast this morning. I'll bring something good tomorrow," she promised, heading over to her favorite seat at the circular table in the middle of the room.

"Don't change the subject on me, Dawn. I've heard about how Hamilton is a ladies' man," Richard said, following her across the room. "He was coming on to you, wasn't he, and you were flirting back with him."

"I wasn't flirting with anyone. Why would I when I have a man like you in my life?" Dawn blew on her coffee and then took a sip. The flavor pushed down some of the anxiety building up in her body. Richard wouldn't like it if he found out Hamilton was trying to steal her away from him. Her boyfriend loved the thrill of competition, but she wasn't a prize to be won.

"You aren't going to tell me what that call was about, are you?" he asked, grabbing a muffin out of the box before he sat down next to her.

"See, you don't know me as well as you think you do," she sighed, placing the mug on the table. "Hamilton emailed me a list of liquors he thought might be good assets to *D4*. He even offered to let us taste a few before we made a final decision," Dawn continued. "I only called him to thank him for being so generous with his time and resources."

For an instant, his eyes sharpened as his gaze locked with hers. "But I bet he wanted a different kind of thank you," Richard accused.

Men. Richard overheard one little phone call, and now he thinks I'm cheating on him.

"Do you think I'm cheating on you with Hamilton Madsen?" Dawn asked, dropping her eyes as she picked the walnuts off her muffin, tossing them back into her box. "Do you think I'm the type of women to sleep with him to get us extra stuff?"

Richard's hand shot across the table and stopped her picking. "Look at me," he murmured. He didn't continue talking until her eyes rose back up to his. "I'm sorry. I shouldn't have said that to you. It's just that I'm horny and jumped on you because of it." He offered her a contrite smile and waited.

She loved how Richard voiced how much he wanted her. He was so different from the Richard in the past that constantly hid his feelings from her. A soft and loving curve touched Dawn's lips as her gaze flirted back with the man in front of her. "If we weren't at work, I would take care of that problem for you."

"Don't let work stop you," Richard growled, pulling her up from her seat. "I'm all yours. Have your way with me."

"Baby, I wish that I could but I have a lunch date, and I have to keep it," she sighed, removing his hands from her body. "But I'll make it up to you tonight at your house."

Linking his hands behind her back, Richard slid her between his legs until her chest touched his. "Cancel your lunch plans, and we can pick something up for lunch, go home and spend the rest of the day in bed making love," he suggested, massaging her back. "You always have lunch plans. Can't you get rid of them this one time for me?"

She would love to spend the rest of the day making love to Richard, but she had to give Johnny some of the money that he wanted. After his threat to visit Hamilton, he was getting desperate for money, and she had to find a way to stop him. "How about this: I'll go to this meeting, and afterwards, I'll stop by that new Chinese place and grab us something."

Richard regarded her with a speculative stare, and her heart started to pound in her chest. What if he turned her idea down? She didn't have the extra time to go another round with him today.

"How long do you think you'll be?" he asked, moving her back so he could stand up.

"Thirty minutes, an hour tops," she answered, swinging around to snatch her purse off the chair. Sliding it on her shoulder, she turned back around and brushed her lips across Richard's as she spoke. "I promise after this, I'll try to cut back on the lunch meetings."

Richard wrapped his hand around her arm and used the back of his free hand to stroke her cheek. "If you needed my help for anything, would you would ask me? I'm not only talking about *D4*, but anything you're having difficulties with."

She was certain now that she was in love with him. How could she keep what was going on with Johnny from him any longer? Richard was being open and honest with her, yet this wasn't his battle to fight or get rid of. "Baby, thank you for the offer, but this isn't something you need to worry about." Standing on tiptoes, she touched her lips to his and murmured, "I love you, Richard Drace." Dawn moved back quickly and left the room before he could answer her.

* * * *

Richard waited until Dawn was completely out of the room before he raced over to the desk and picked up the phone. He didn't give the person on the other end a chance to say hello before he uttered, "She's leaving. Be sure to stay with her until she comes back to *D4*. Yes, I know what I am doing. Let me go, or you're going to miss her." He hung up the phone and sat down on the edge of his desk. "Dawn, I'm going to find out who you are meeting and put an end to it."

Chapter Twenty-Five

"Here's some of your money, you bastard," Dawn hissed, tossing the envelope at Johnny. "I had to cash in some bonds to get that damn money for you."

"Oh, Dawny, don't be mad at me," Johnny slurred, trying to stand upright. "You know that if I didn't crave the drugs, I wouldn't ask you for the money." A dirt-covered hand shoved the thick brown envelope inside a denim jacket pocket. "This will keep me in the coke for a while."

"It better, because I don't have anymore to give you," Dawn snapped, looking around the parking lot to make sure no one was watching them, because she had this bad feeling someone was. "Now give me that tape and I'm out of here."

Johnny grinned at her, displaying another missing tooth in his once-perfect mouth. "I can't do that."

"Why not? I kept up with my end of the bargain," she said. "It's only fair that you give me that tape."

Johnny's hand scratched at his scalp, and she took a step back from all of the filth that fell on his shoulders. She had to find a way to get rid of Johnny before he ruined what she had with Richard. "You look so bad. Why don't you join a treatment clinic and get yourself straight? You were one the smartest guys in high school. Didn't you rank number thirty-two out of a class of one hundred and forty-seven?"

Pulling his hand out of his hair, Johnny flicked the dirt from under his fingernails and then wiped them on his denim jacket. "That was a long time ago. Time changes, and so do people, as you should know," Johnny spat, his voice heavy with sarcasm. "You dumped me the second you laid eyes on that restaurant guy."

"I'm not going to go down this road with you again, but I will this one last time. We weren't a couple."

"Yes, we were."

"No, we weren't, Johnny, and you know it," Dawn exclaimed, taking a quick peek at her watch. "I need to go, or I'm going to be late for another appointment, but I want that tape, and you won't get any more money until I get it." Spinning on her heel, she got into her car, slammed the door and drove off.

Dawn kept driving until she got about two blocks from the library parking lot; then she parked her car under a shade tree and dropped her head on the wheel. She was tired of dealing with Johnny on top of all the extra things she was juggling at D4. It was beginning to take a toll on her body. Last night, she only got about three hours' sleep before she was up and working on a good investment plan for Richard. When she was done with D4, it would be the hottest place in Texas, and Richard would finally respect her.

Taking a calming breath, she started the car and headed to the Chinese restaurant for the early dinner that she promised Richard. At least she had him for this short period of time, because before he knew it, she would be gone and back out there looking for a new job.

* * * *

"What did you find out? Is Dawn in some kind of trouble that I need to know about?"

Richard stood outside his place of business, waiting for his youngest brother to stop staring at him and answer his question. Dawn wasn't telling him something, and he wanted to know what it was.

"I had to skip out on a lunch date with Alicia to do this for you," Brad complained, a strong edge to his voice. "The first time in months that Alicia is free for lunch, and I couldn't go with her."

"I'm sorry, okay?" Richard sighed. "I'll pay for a night out on the town with your reporter if you tell me what you found out about Dawn."

"I don't know if I should tell you or not," Brad hedged.

"Tell me. I have to meet Dawn at my house for an early dinner." Richard watched as a still yet serious expression passed over Brad's usually relaxed face.

"Dawn met this guy in the parking lot of the library and handed him a thick brown envelope. The guy shoved it into his pocket, then they argued back and forth for a minute or two. After she left, the guy stayed in the parking lot for about two minutes, then he got in his car and drove off."

"What did he look like?" he asked, wondering if it was the same guy from Dawn's apartment a few weeks back.

"Skinny, with long, dirty, blond hair and tattered clothes," Brad answered. "I was surprised that Dawn even knew someone like that. She doesn't seem like the type to hang around riffraff."

"She isn't," he agreed, not comprehending how worried his voice sounded.

"Do you want me to follow her tomorrow?" Brad asked.

"I'm not sure yet," Richard replied. "I have to call and let you know."

"I still think you need to be up front and ask Dawn what's going on. You know how sensitive she can be sometimes about the way you treat her," Brad exclaimed.

"I'm not doing anything to hurt her this time," Richard remarked, upset that Brad was on Dawn's side instead of his. "Dawn knows that I love her."

"Does she?"

"Listen, I'm going to leave before we get into a fight. I'm sorry that you missed out on having lunch with Alicia. Tell her it was my fault." Richard didn't have the patience to stick around and hear the rest of what his brother had to say. He got into his car and left.

* * * *

The soft flickering of lights coming from inside his house caught Richard's attention the second he parked his car inside the circular driveway. Getting out, he pressed the alarm on his keychain and then sauntered to the front door. Richard waited until he got inside and locked the door before he called out to Dawn.

"Dawn, where are you?" Richard spotted several lit candles scattered through the foyer. The light scent of vanilla, mingled with an unfamiliar yet sexy scent, filled his nose and stirred his crotch. Tossing his keys on the table next to the door, he picked up the folded pink note card that was lying next to a picture of his parents. He flicked it open and smiled at Dawn's perfect writing.

Hello baby,

I thought you might like to participate in Dawn's search-and-find, my naughty twist on hide-and-go-seek. I have left little clues around the house to where I am hiding. When you find the right place, there will be a note attached, giving you a clue to my next location. However, if you don't guess correctly, there will be a note, but without a clue to my next spot.

Now strip down and make your first guess. I'll be waiting for you, so hurry up and find me.

Love,
Dawn

Richard tore off his clothes until he was standing there barefoot and wearing only his favorite pair of jeans. He couldn't stop the rush of blood to his penis at the thought of Dawn, somewhere in his house, waiting for him, naked. Hell, he would take her in something skimpy, if she would let him strip it from her toned body. All he wanted was the chance to spend another night in the arms of the woman he loved more with each passing day.

"Dawn, I hope that you can hear me because this is the last warning I'm going to give you," he yelled through his quiet house. "The game is about to start, so you better be ready. I'm still horny as hell, and I want to spend the night making love to you until both of us are too weak to do it any more."

Rubbing his hands together, he cleared his mind and then thought about the first place Dawn's next note could be. His feisty girlfriend loved so many things in his home, but she always talked about the statue of the cougar by the fireplace. Leaving the vestibule, he kept moving until he stopped in front of the sculpture, and there, attached to the head, was a note card.

Good job, sweetie,
Now you're a step closer to me, and my body is getting all wet with excitement. Keep going, and I promise it will be worth it.
Dawn

Bringing the card to his nose, he breathed in the sweet aroma and then tossed it back by the cougar, he couldn't waste his time on a piece of paper when Dawn was waiting for him somewhere inside his house.

He paused and took a breath. "Where else in this place would she leave a message for me?" Richard didn't have a clue in hell where the next hint could be, but he wasn't going to let that stop him from guessing.

Chapter Twenty-Six

The silence of the house ate at him as he eased from one room to another, without finding another note. Richard thought that he had Dawn pretty well figured out when it came to his house. Hell, he was confident enough to even say that he knew her like the back of his hand; however, he was beginning to doubt his natural instincts. Dawn was playing with him, and he loved it.

His shy little kitten had turned into a full-fledged seductress with this game of hers, and he couldn't wait to see where the next clue would lead him. Rubbing his hands together, Richard thought he was going to flip the page in his favor later on. Dawn might have him now, but she would be his in every sense of the word before the night was over.

Heading into the kitchen, he grinned the second his gaze landed on a pink note card leaning against a bowl of strawberries, with a jar of chocolate syrup next to it. Going across the room, he picked up the card and quickly scanned it.

Baby, you are on a roll, and this pleases me.
You're getting so close to me.
I can't almost feel your hands on my body.

One more card to go, and then I can give you a big hint where to find your treasure.
Your kitten,
Dawn

Tossing the message down on the table, Richard picked up the dessert Dawn had planned for them and hurried from the room; he didn't even need to go looking for the last clue. He already knew where Dawn was waiting for him. He felt so stupid that he hadn't thought of it earlier.

"She better be ready for me, because I know that I'm more than prepared to give her everything she wants and more," he said, rushing towards the back of the house.

Richard slowed down when he got to the very back of his house and then slipped through the open game room entrance. Inch by inch, he made his way to the patio doors that led to his fenced-in yard. He had the fence installed about two years ago because he hated how nosy his neighbors were.

The strawberries and syrup almost dropped from his hands and crashed to the tile floor when he spotted Dawn over by the hot rub wearing next to nothing. The dark brown bikini blended in so perfectly with her natural skin. He had to do a double take to make sure she wasn't naked.

Pushing the door open wider with his arm, he shouldered his way through and kept his eyes on the prize as he snuck over to Dawn. He wasn't about to let that tempting body of hers go to waste any longer. As he got closer to her, he realized that her eyes were closed. She didn't have a clue he had already found her. Pausing by the picnic table, Richard set the 'play later' items down before he continued on his way.

His lower body stirred and grew harder in the confines of his pants as the sweet scent of Dawn's body drifted towards him. He hated to bother her because he loved the sight of her stretched across the back of the hot tub. Somehow over the past few weeks, the Dawn he had chased out of his office six months ago had disappeared, only to be replaced by this goddess in front of him. He wasn't complaining. The new Dawn had an air of calm and self-confidence, which he liked. She stood up to him now, instead of keeping everything bottled up.

As he got closer to his sexy manager, it occurred to him that his eyes were riveted to her face; he slipped them over the bare skin exposed by the skimpy swimsuit. He was almost close enough now that he could run his fingers over the smooth skin. Just as Richard reached out to touch the side of Dawn's navel, a soft voice stopped him.

"You don't play fair," Dawn whispered, opening her eyes. She turned her head and directed her steady gaze into his eyes.

"Why would you say that?" he asked, brushing his fingers over her taut stomach.

"Because you skipped my last note and came straight out here. I should be so mad at you," Dawn pouted, moving his hand off her body.

"Are you upset with me?" he questioned, replacing his hand back on skin. "After I figured out where you were, I couldn't stay away from you."

"Why?"

"Why, what?" Richard mumbled as his fingers unhooked the front clasp on her suit.

"Why couldn't you stay away from me?" she asked, raising her body so Richard could take off her bikini top. He tossed it on the ground and then brushed the palms of his hands over her hard nipples. Small electrical currents shot through her body as he kept one hand on her breast. He slowly undid her bottoms, slipping his other hand between her legs.

"Because I knew that you would be like this," Richard said, drawing two fingers in and out of her.

"H-how am I?" she stammered, biting her bottom lip to keep her moans at bay.

"Wet and ready for me," he answered, removing his thick fingers from her throbbing body. Without removing his eyes from her face, Richard stood up at the side of the hot tub and removed the rest of his clothing.

"Get up and stand down here, at the other side of me."

* * * *

He waited while she got out of the hot tub and stood next to him. She felt her skin come alive with the way Richard's eyes smoldered with fire and ownership. In the past, she hadn't when men looked at her like that, but it felt totally different when Richard showed her the same attention. It made her burn with the need to have him buried deep within her body.

Richard sat on the middle step and spread his legs. "Come here," he whispered, wiggling his index finger at her.

"What do you want?" She stepped toward Richard and laughed when he grabbed her wrist and tugged her to him.

"This," Richard growled as he lifted her up over his erection and thrust into her waiting body.

Purring, she wrapped her arms around Richard's shoulders and let him control the movements of her body. Dawn didn't know where her soul started and his ended. Each and every time she made love with Richard, he stole another piece of her willpower to leave him.

She gasped when Richard got up from the step and carried her over to the loungers by the patio doors. "I need more room to make love to you," he whispered by her ear before he placed her body on the largest one. Wrapping his hands around her hips, Richard maintained a steady rhythm as his body endlessly loved her.

As his head dropped to her chest, a moist tongue darted out and caressed one swollen nipple, making it harder and more in need of attention. After a second or two, the magic tongue showed her left nipple the same attention.

"Oh," she moaned, arching her back, giving Richard more breasts to love.

"I feel it too, Kitten," Richard breathed, flexing his hips, going even deeper into her body. Lips and tongue made a searing path down her ribs, over her stomach, and then back up to her mouth for a sizzling, open-mouthed kiss.

She matched his uncontrollable urgency with her own unabashed needs until the tingling sensation started in the base of her spine. The orgasm hit her so quickly, she only had time to latch on to Richard's shoulders and hold on for the ride. Dawn was so caught up in her own release that she almost missed out on Richard's screams of pleasure the second before all his weight collapsed on her body.

Chapter Twenty-Seven

"You look way too happy this morning," Brad commented, staring at the smile on Richard's face. "What have you been up to?"

Richard fixed the pencil holder on Brad's oak desk and then leaned back in the leather seat before he replied. "I've fallen in love with the most wonderful woman in the world."

"Oh, so Emily finally wore you down enough to make you fall for her," his brother joked.

"You know damn well I'm not talking about Emily," he snapped. "I haven't seen that pest in weeks, and I couldn't be happier. Dawn is the woman I'm referring to."

"I know she is," Brad chuckled. "I was only kidding with you. Does Dawn know she has her small hand wrapped around your heart yet?"

"I have done everything to show how much I care about her."

"Showing her and telling her are two different things," Brad sighed. "If I thought telling Alicia I was in love with her would win her over, I'll do it in a hot second."

Richard stopped thinking about himself for a moment, shocked that Brad was falling for a woman who didn't care a thing about him. "Why are you still so attracted to Alicia? She hasn't even shown any romantic interest in you."

"How can you sit there and judge me when Dawn hated you for the longest time? I still don't know you got her to come back after all the horrible things you said about her," Brad tossed back at him.

Shit, he hated when Brad was right and he was wrong. "You're right, man. I have no room to pass my opinions on to you when I wasn't good to Dawn in the beginning. However, all of that has changed now, and I would do anything for her."

"Can't you see that's how I feel about Alicia?" his brother questioned, holding his gaze across the desk. "I see her looking at me when she doesn't think I'm looking at her. She just has to get over this crush she has on Max."

"Do you think it's possible? What if Max starts to return her feelings?"

"Alicia is mine!" Brad snapped, slamming his hand down on his furniture. "I've been in love with her longer than you have known Dawn. She just needs time to get over the hero worship."

"Hero worship?" he said, confused by his brother's choice of words.

"Max helped her land the job at the news station, and ever since then, she's been in lust with him," Brad said.

"Are you sure it's just lust?" Richard inquired.

"Yes, it's just lust. If it was more, Alicia wouldn't have enjoyed the kiss we shared at the tennis court."

Grinning, Richard nodded, "I remember that day. Alicia ran past me like the hounds of hell were after her."

"Well, I wouldn't compare myself to the hounds of hell, but I am a man determined to get the woman I want," Brad said, with passion shining from his peacock eyes. "I have learned how to stay persistent from Lee."

Richard hadn't talked to Lee in a couple of days, so he wasn't up to date on the next stage in Lee's plan to win over their spunky sister-in-law's sister. Cherise Roberts captivated Lee the first time he laid eyes on her, and it hadn't changed. However, Cherise wasn't falling for any of his brother's charm or stolen kisses. She pretended Lee was a stranger instead of part of her immediate family. "What's going on now with the two of them?" he queried.

"Traci invited Cherise over to dinner last night, leaving out that Zack also gave an invitation to Lee and me," Brad said. "You should have seen her face the second she turned the corner and spotted Lee. I thought she was going to turn around and leave."

"She actually stayed?"

"Yeah, and here's the shocker. Cherise sat beside Lee and had a civilized conversation."

"You're kidding me," Richard uttered shocked. "Hell, I would've loved to see that."

"Hey, Zack invited you, too, but you had better things to do than spend it with your family," Brad responded, giving him a look. "I don't have to guess how you were spending your time."

"No, you don't. I was with Dawn and loving every minute of it. God, you don't know how much I care about her. She is the secret ingredient that has been missing from my life."

"Does that mean you're going to stop having me follow her?" Brad tossed out, crashing his euphoria down around his feet.

He hated that Dawn still didn't love him enough to come clean with that certain part of her life. He couldn't let it go until he knew exactly what was going on. "No, I still want you to follow her. I have to know why she keeps meeting with that guy, and she isn't about to tell me."

"I still think this is a bad idea. Just ask her, and I'm sure Dawn will tell you the truth."

"I can't chance her finding out that you're following her. No, I'll do it this way for a little while longer," Richard stated. "If I don't find out what she's doing in a couple of days, I'll follow her myself and get the answers from him."

"This is going to blow up in your face. Dawn is going to be hurt you did this to her," Brad commented. "Take my advice; ask Dawn and see where it goes from there."

"I didn't come here seeking your opinion," Richard countered. "I only want you to do as I ask and nothing more."

"Fine. I can do that."

"Good, that's all I want," Richard retorted, standing to leave. "I have a late lunch appointment with a vendor, so I'll call you later."

"You're working on a Saturday, too?" Brad asked.

"I have to if I want to have *D4* back up and running," Richard said.

* * * *

Outside his brother's office, Richard pulled out his cell phone and then pressed one on the speed dial.

"Dawn Summers speaking."

"Kitten, I guess you're with someone, since you're answering the phone in your business voice."

"How can I help you, Mr. Drace?"

"You can cut your meeting short and meet me back at my house. I want to get a chance to use that chocolate syrup."

"Oh, I'm sorry that offer expired last night, and a refund wasn't part of the deal."

"You didn't tell me that last night," he complained. "If I had known, we wouldn't have gone that last round in the hot tub."

"I did try, but you had other plans," Dawn tossed back. "If my memory serves me correctly, I brought it up when we were on the lounger that third time."

He smiled at the memory of giving Dawn her third release last night, using only his fingers. It would be something that he would never forget. "Are you sure I can't find a way to get another shot at the strawberries-and-syrup offer? I promise it won't lapse a second time."

"I'm sorry, Mr. Drace. That offer is over. But I'm open to another similar deal if you can come up with another one," Dawn suggested. "But I'm with a client at the moment, so I'll talk to you later. Thanks for calling."

Richard moved the cell phone away from his ear as the dial tone came on and stared at it. Dawn knew better than to leave their next romantic encounter up to him. He would have her shouting his name the instant his mouth latched onto one of those perfect nipples of hers.

Shoving the phone back into his suit pocket, he was already thinking of ways to make Dawn surrender to him later that night. She wouldn't be able to leave him or his bed once when his gentle loving was over.

* * * *

"Sorry about that," Dawn apologized, sliding her cell phone back into her purse. "Mr. Drace had a question for me that just couldn't wait."

"I would be checking up on you, too, if you were out on a date with another man," Hamilton replied, taking a sip of his orange juice.

When would Hamilton stop flirting with her? He knew she was in a relationship with Richard, but this man had no self-control. She couldn't believe how easily these comments came from his lips. "You know this isn't a date, Hamilton."

"Can't you let a guy dream?"

"You can dream all you want, just don't let Richard find out that you are," she tossed back, wishing that Richard would care that Hamilton enjoyed making her feel wanted.

"Drace would be a fool if he let someone as gorgeous as you slip through his fingers."

"How about we stay on the topic I came here for? *D4* is interested in inquiring several of the liquors that you emailed to me," Dawn stated. She pulled a list out of the side of her purse and slid it over to Hamilton. "I made a list of the items and the quantity. Do you think you can have it ready by the time we want to open?"

Hamilton picked up her list. He read over it a couple of times before he laid it back down on the table. "I don't think it should be a problem filling this order for you. Have you thought about adding some cocktails to the list, too? I know some people don't like the other liquors I offered you."

"Cocktails? What kind?" she questioned.

"More aimed towards the female customers that might come in for a ladies' night."

"That's a good idea. I'll run it past Richard," Dawn said, writing it down in her notebook. "Why are you helping me out so much? I know you have interests in several other restaurants around here. D4 is almost like your competition in some ways."

Hamilton studied her, and then a grin took over his features. "I'm a liquor merchant first, and I'll place my liquor anywhere that will give me more business. But my attraction to you is a little selfish. I want you in my new restaurant and my bed."

"You shouldn't be telling me this," she answered in a voice that didn't sound like her own. It was low and soft, almost like a whisper.

"I'm an honest man, and I can't lie about the temptation you are to me. Do you know how many times I have woken up hard from dreaming about you?"

Dawn quickly picked up her things off the table, shoving them into her purse. "Hamilton, you know I can't go there with you. I care about Richard, and you know that. I don't like you have placed me in this uncomfortable position. I think Mr. Drace should deal with future business meetings when it comes to you." She rushed past the table as Hamilton tossed a handful of bills down on it.

She had almost made it to her car when Hamilton wrapped his hand around her arm and twirled her back around. His mouth landed on hers before she could get one word out of her mouth. She kept her mouth closed and waited until Hamilton realized she wasn't responding to him.

He slowly let go of her arm and took several steps back. "Dawn, I'm sorry that I did that, but I've been wondering what it would be like to kiss you for weeks. I can promise you it won't happen again, and I hope I haven't lost *D4*'s business."

"Why couldn't you take my word that I wasn't interested in a relationship with you?" she questioned, touching her lips with the tips of her fingers. "Don't you know that you can't go around kissing women who don't want it?"

"I do now," Hamilton answered. "Does this mean I lost the deal I have with Richard?"

Dawn wanted more than anything to yell and scream at the sexy man in front of her, but she had a small part in letting Hamilton think he could kiss her. She didn't make her feelings for Richard clear enough in the past, but she would do so now.

"Hamilton, I'm in love with Richard, and I think he's beginning to care about me, too. I don't want to do anything to jeopardize what is blooming between us. I'll let you keep the contract on one condition."

"What's the condition?"

"You keep the rest of our meetings about business only. No more personal questions or comments. If it's not about *D4*, don't let it leave your mouth. Do we have a deal?"

"We have a deal," Hamilton agreed. "And I apologize again for overstepping my bounds like that. Are you going to tell Richard about it?"

"Of course I am," Dawn responded. "It's better if he hears it from me than someone else who might have seen us."

Chapter Twenty-Eight

"I don't want you to have any more meetings with Madsen," Richard demanded, storming past her over to the window in his office. "Hell, how can I trust him to deliver the liquor we need, if I can't trust him to keep his hands off of you?" He was beyond mad. Hamilton Madsen was in for a fight the second he spotted the other man out on the street. Why hadn't he put a stop to Dawn meeting with the asshole the second he figured out the other man wanted his woman?

"Don't tell me what to do," Dawn clamored. "I've never told you who you can and can't see, have I?"

"So, you wouldn't care if I found Emily and stuck my tongue halfway down her throat?" Richard fumed, facing her. "Or better, let how about I make love to her on the lounger like I did to you last night?"

Hot tears burned Dawn's eyes as she listened to Richard fling lovemaking with Emily up in her face. He didn't care about her like she thought, or he wouldn't hurt her like this. Once again, she was the pawn in the game he was playing with Emily. Shit, she was tired of going back and forth like this.

Richard had shown his last hand to her, and she wasn't about to let him see her cry.

"Well, now I guess we know where we stand with each other," Dawn stated. "I wondered how long it would be before you grew tired of me and ran back to that slut Emily."

"Wait one minute," Richard growled, hurrying over to her. "I was only making a statement. You know that I don't want Emily over you. How could you even think that after the amazing time we shared last night?"

He reached out to touch her face, but she stepped back from him. "Don't touch me." She would lose her lunch if Richard's hands touched any part of her body. "I don't want to hear you. You have already said enough to keep me up most of the night."

"Dawn, don't do this. You know I couldn't touch another woman after we started making love," Richard pleaded. "Let's go back to my house. I can make us a nice romantic dinner, and we can talk. There's something I need to tell you."

"I'm sorry. I can't," Dawn muttered, turning away from him.

Richard opened his mouth to tell Dawn they weren't finished talking, but his phone rang, cutting him off. "Don't you dare leave this room," he got out before he checked the caller ID and answered the call.

"Zack, this better be really important."

"Traci is in labor, and she's at the hospital. Come here right now," Zack uttered in his ear before he hung up.

A huge grin spread across his face. He was about to become an uncle for the first time. He couldn't think of a better person to share the news with than Dawn. "That's was Zack on the phone. Traci has gone into labor, and he wants the whole family there with him."

"Congrats. You better hurry up. I don't want to make you late."

"You aren't going with me?" he asked as he headed for the door. What was wrong with her? Zack wouldn't care if she came along. Hell, he'd be more stunned if he showed up without her.

"I'm not part of the family. I'm only your employee," Dawn exclaimed, brushing past him before she rushed out the door.

Richard wanted to go after Dawn and make her stand still until she listened to him, but Zack needed him at the hospital. After he got to see his new nephew and hold him, his next stop would be Dawn's house. He wasn't about to go to bed tonight without Dawn wrapped in his arms, knowing how much he loved her.

"Kitten, you're more than my employee," he whispered, going out the door and closing it behind him, "and before the night is over, I'm going to prove it to you."

* * * *

"You know, we're forever connected now since Traci had the baby," Lee said, standing by Cherise, looking through the nursery window at his adorable new nephew. The little boy had both parents' features, so he was going to be very good-looking.

"Do you always have to ruin something?" Cherise asked, not taking her eyes off the sleeping baby.

"Oh, you know that you're enjoying this time alone with me," Lee chuckled, wrapping his arm around Cherise's shoulder. "You did volunteer to come down here with me."

"Don't read more into it than there is," Cherise sighed, brushing off his arm. "Zack wanted to stay upstairs with Traci until Richard got here, and I wanted to see my nephew."

"Do you think our baby will look that cute?" Lee questioned by Cherise's ear. He smiled when her body jerked before she took a step away from him.

"When you have a baby, it sure won't be with me," she hissed, swinging her head ,glaring at him with her beautiful colored eyes. Cherise could glower at him all she wanted, as long as she kept talking to him. Half the time she acted like he was a stranger to her instead a part of her family.

"Cherise, I want a baby, and I don't want anyone else to be the mother but you. So, what do you say? How about allowing me to give you some extra special attention tonight? Who knows? Nine months from today, we could be standing here smiling at our little boy or girl."

"I can't wait to hear the answer to this. Yeah, what do you say, Cherise? Are you going to let my brother be your baby's daddy?" Richard's rich voice laughed, interrupting their conversation.

Richard better be glad we're in a hospital, or I would strangle him within an inch of his life, Lee thought as he watched Cherise slam another door in the way of winning her over. At the rate his plan was going, Brad would be married to Alicia before he got Cherise to admit she had feelings for him.

"Richard, I'm not staying here, so you and your juvenile brother can pick on me. I'm going back upstairs to visit with my sister," Cherise said, brushing past him and Lee.

"Great, you scared her off," Lee muttered, watching the sway of Cherise's round hips in a tight pair of jeans as she practically ran from them. "I might have talked her into it."

"Please come back from that planet you're living on, big brother," Richard snickered. "Cherise doesn't want you within twenty feet of her. How can you actually think she'll let you father her child?"

"Just wait and see. I'm going to have Cherise along with every wonderful thing that comes with it," Lee promised as he stole another glance down at the newest addition to the Drace family.

Chapter Twenty-Nine

"Dawn, open the door. I know that you're in there, Kitten." Richard knocked on the door for the third time in the span of ten minutes. "I'm not going to leave tonight until we talk about what happened today at D4. You know I don't want any other woman but you. Please come to the door."

"Sir, you can keep knocking on her door all night, but she isn't going to answer," a voice uttered behind him.

Turning around, Richard spotted a young boy in a baseball jersey, staring at him from the sidewalk. He would have guessed the kid was around thirteen, maybe fourteen years old. "Do you know where Dawn is?"

"Yeah, she left with some man about two hours ago."

He wondered whether it was Hamilton or the man Dawn had been meeting every day for lunch for the past eight weeks. "Can you describe what the man looked like?'

"Why do you want to know? Are you her boyfriend or something?"

"Yes, I am, and I need to talk to her."

"You're a liar because Miss Summers doesn't have a boyfriend," the boy replied, giving him an odd look. "Are you a stalker or something? I saw a program on television about how men harassed unsuspecting females. I like Miss Summers. She helps me with my history homework when I need it."

He could tell that the young man had a slight crush on Dawn, and he didn't blame him. Dawn was a beautiful woman. A man would have to be crazy not to fall in love with her the second he laid eyes on her.

"You're right. I'm not really her boyfriend." Why should he hurt the boy's feelings? "I'm her boss, Richard Drace, and I need to talk to her about a work-related matter. Are you sure you can't help me find her?"

Richard watched the boy act like a heavy weight had been lifted off his shoulders. "Oh, I know who you are now. You called her house once while she was tutoring me last week. I guess it will be all right to tell you where she went to."

"Yes, Dawn wouldn't want to miss the message I have to give her," Richard agreed.

"Her and the guy went back to the restaurant. I overheard them talking about some floor plans for the place. I think, but I'm not sure. I was trying to get Dawn's attention, but I don't think she saw me."

"Thanks for the information." Richard hurried down the steps, not stopping when the boy tried to ask him another question. He had to get to *D4* and make sure Dawn wasn't trying to avoid him.

* * * *

"Can you really have the remodeling done that fast?"

"Sure, the foundations for both buildings are amazing. I thought it might take me longer, but eight weeks should be plenty of time to connect the two."

Dawn came out of the building next door to *D4* with David Cody, the contractor she hired to do the revisions on the extra space. "Have I told you how much I appreciate that you came down here at the last minute?" she asked, locking the door behind them.

"Hey, I wasn't doing anything at home. Besides, I used to come into *D4* all the time when it was up and running," David said. "I'm more than happy to help get the doors open again."

"Let me run all of this past Mr. Drace first. He has the final say, and if it's okay with him, then I'll give you a call." Dawn walked beside David as they made their way back to *D4*.

"Are the rumors true?"

"What rumors?" Dawn unlocked *D4* and let David go in. Then she went in after him.

"That Richard is lucky enough to call you his girlfriend?" David inquired.

She couldn't control her burst of laughter. What was with all these men coming on to her? She never had much attention until after people believed that she was 'an item' with Richard. "No, that isn't true. I'm not dating Mr. Drace. We are just friends."

"Dawn, you shouldn't lie to the man," Richard said, coming through the kitchen with a pair of keys dangling from his fingers. "You know that we've been in a relationship for weeks now."

God, when would she get a break from this merry-go-round that Richard called their relationship? One minute he was tossing Emily in her face, and then in the next, he wanted to hit Hamilton, and now probably David, for taking to her.

David reached past her and offered his hand to Richard. "Nice to see you again, Richard. I was going over the plans I had for *D4*."

"Same here, man," Richard answered, dropping David's hand. Then his eyes landed on Dawn. Circling his arm around her waist, Richard planted a kiss below her ear. "Hello, Kitten. I missed you." She tried to control the trembling of her body but couldn't.

Kitten.

Dawn felt Richard's fingers stroking underneath her breast and hated how much her body responded to him. "I don't think you should call me that. It might give Mr. Cody the wrong idea about us."

Richard's hand tightened on her waist. "Dawn, everyone in this town knows you're my woman, David here included. We went to high school and college together. David knows I don't give up anything without a fight."

"You haven't changed one bit, Rich. Still the ladies' man," David chuckled in front of her. "I can tell that I'm about to be the third wheel, so let me gather my things and I'm out of here."

Before Dawn could unhinge her jaw and ask David to stay so she didn't have to be by herself with Richard, he was already out the door and in his car. The only thing left of David was his headlights fading in the distance.

"What are you doing here?" Dawn loosened Richard's grip and then moved away from him. "I thought you would be at the hospital with your family."

"I'm going back later, but I forgot to do something before I left."

"I can't imagine the great Richard 'Do-No-Wrong' Drace forgot anything," she muttered under her breath.

"Well, I did. Don't you want to know what it was?" he murmured, enveloping her wrist in his hand.

"No."

"Sorry, you're going to," Richard uttered before he swiftly covered her mouth with his. "I'm so sorry for the way I treated you," he breathed by the side of her mouth. "I can't apologize enough for tossing Emily in your face." Moving her back, Richard placed a finger under her chin and tilted her face up. "I swear to you that I only want you. Emily isn't in my life anymore. I lashed out because I was jealous that Hamilton saw the same wonderful qualities in you that I do."

"Next time, just tell me that, instead of shoving me away with your words," she said.

"Does that mean you forgive me?"

"You know I can't ever stay mad at you for a long time." Dawn hated how Richard only had to look at her with those green eyes of his and she was mush in his hands.

"Good, because I would hate for the woman I was in love with to hate the sight of me," Richard mumbled, kissing on her the mouth before he stepped back from her.

Richard loved her!

"You love me?"

"Of course I do. Why do you think I get so riled up when you spend so much time with these other men?" Richard questioned. "Now let's get this place locked up. I want to show you my handsome little nephew. Thank God he took after Traci instead of my brother."

Dawn stood back, still in shock mode after hearing Richard's confession, while he checked the restaurant, making sure everything was in its place. She wanted to be off the wall with happiness. Richard had finally told her the words she longed for, but some of her bliss was tarnished.

Would Richard still love her after he found out about the videotape?

Chapter Thirty

"There's something wrong with Dawn. She isn't acting like herself, and she won't tell me what it is." Brad finished lacing up his tennis shoes and stared at Richard, sitting next to him on the park bench. "I thought you told her that you loved her, like, two weeks ago."

"I did." Richard sighed, folding his hands between his legs. "But she isn't acting like I thought she would. Don't get me wrong. We make love every night, and it's wonderful."

"Then what is exactly is the problem? Do I still need to follow her?"

Richard took his time and thought about Brad's question. Dawn hadn't been on any lunch dates in a while, but she was still hiding something from him. They were two halves of a whole, yet Dawn was making it very hard for them to fit together.

"Yes, I want you to keep following her until I tell you to stop." He hated doing this to her, but Dawn wasn't letting him in. How could he understand her emotions better when he didn't have a clue about her outside the restaurant?

"I'm really beginning not to like this. Dawn is so sweet, and what you're doing to her is so wrong, on so many different levels. You keep saying how much you love her, but having me watch Dawn's every move isn't love," Brad blasted.

"I know it isn't," Richard spouted, getting up from the bench. "Can we drop this for now and finish our run? Dawn is running some last-minute errands, and I want to be home when she gets back."

* * * *

"Can I talk to you?" Dawn slid the strap of her purse back onto her shoulder as she watched Zack place his son back into the bassinet. "I don't have anyone else to turn to."

Zack brushed his son's hair off his forehead and looked over at her. "Dawn, come in and have a seat. Tell me, what has my brother done to you this time? Do you want to me to have a talk with him? Or are you here about *D4*?"

Coming into the room, Dawn closed the door behind her and sat down in a chair. "This isn't about *D4*, and Richard has been the most loving boyfriend a woman could ask for. It's me. I have done something, and I'm afraid if Richard finds out, he'll hate me for the rest of my life."

Zack tried to hide his surprise, but she saw it as he took a seat. "It can't be bad as you're making it out to be. Richard loves you and will stand by you no matter what."

Dawn looked back at Richard's brother for the longest time without speaking. She didn't know why she had come here in the first place. How could she tell Zack her secret before Richard? He was her boyfriend and deserved to know, but she didn't have the strength to do it.

"Let me tell you my secret, and after you hear the whole story, I want you tell me again how much Richard still loves me."

Rubbing her hands together, Dawn blew on them a couple of times, trying to gather up her courage. "You remember how much I cared about your brother when I worked for him. I think everyone in town knew I was in love with Richard but him. My heart would lodge in my throat every time he paid the slightest bit of attention to me.

"I thought that maybe if I spent more time around him, he might start seeing me more and ask me out on a date. I went to work every day hoping it would be the day Richard Drace finally saw what was in front of his gorgeous face, but it didn't happen. He thought I was acting like a school girl with a crush and lashed out at me."

"Yeah, Richard told us about that incident over dinner," Zack interjected. "You still don't know how sorry he is."

"Richard will regret feeling sorry for me, and you'll be disgusted with me after I finish telling you the rest of my story."

"Why don't you let me be the judge of that?"

She shrugged off Zack's comment and continued with her story. "Well, I was feeling worthless and very unattractive. I kept thinking if Richard didn't want me, why would any other man? I had to prove I was attractive enough to get someone."

"What did you do?"

"When I first moved out here, I came with my best friend and ex-boyfriend, Johnny. We were like two peas in a bowl of pea soup. We did everything with each other, until Johnny got a drug habit and I broke things off with him. I couldn't have him in my life with a cocaine habit."

"What does Johnny have to do with this secret you're keeping from my brother?" Zack asked.

Her stomach started to ache at the thought of finally allowing her secret out in the open. Zack would tell Richard to leave her so quickly after hearing her confession, but she went on.

"I ran into Johnny about a week after Richard kicked me out of D4. He was in the park panhandling. He ran out of money pretty quick, so he had to find ways to earn more to keep from going through withdrawal.

"I didn't want to talk to him, but he kept following me around, bugging me, until I broke down and told him what happened. That's when I first about the Pleasure Pal."

"The Pleasure Pal," Zack muttered. "I have never heard of the place."

"Be glad that you haven't. God, I wished Johnny never gave me that purple and gold card," Dawn sighed, dropping her hands down into her lap. "It turned out to be the beginning of the end for me."

"Go on and tell me the rest."

She breathed in shallow, quick gasps before she raised her head. "The Pleasure Pal is located near the end of town because the men there don't want their families finding out about them. It's always filled with doctors, lawyers, judges and anyone else with hand-over-fist money. They all want their secret pleasures fulfilled, but there's only one catch."

"What's the catch?" Zack's voice jumped in.

"All of them only want young, attractive black women to perform for them."

"Dawn, what did you do?"

Thinking back now, she knew what she was doing at the time was wrong, but she had to find out if Richard's words were true. Why hadn't she listened to her first instinct and go back home? She had Richard now, but she might end up losing him in the end.

"My client had a fetish for...," she paused, getting choked up at the memory.

"You don't have to tell me this if you don't want to," Zack said, his voice breaking through her pain.

"No, I have to tell someone, or I'll go crazy." Dawn wiped the tears away from the corners of her eyes and then pushed on. "My client had a fetish for licking certain parts of a woman's body. The more he got to lick you, the more excited he became until he came."

"Did you ever have sex with any of these men?"

"Sex wasn't a part of the fantasy when it came to them. They wanted to do things with you and to you that their wives wouldn't let them do." Chewing her bottom lip, Dawn wondered if she should tell Zack the rest.

"There's more, isn't there?"

"I didn't know the most popular girls got taped for future training sessions for the new girls. One of Johnny's buddies worked at the Pleasure Pal, and he stole the tape of me for Johnny. He has been blackmailing me with it for drug money."

"Tell Richard about this. He won't dump you. Hell, he'll blame himself for sending you to a place like that in the first place. Honey, my brother is so in love with you. He loved you when he yelled at you all those months ago, but the idiot was too arrogant to realize it."

"I don't know," Dawn said, shaking her head. "Richard goes crazy when I tell him about Hamilton Madsen flirting with me. How can I confess this to him?"

"Tell him before Johnny gets desperate and makes it worse than it is. Your friend sounds very dangerous. Let Richard help you get rid of this mess."

"No, this is my problem, and I can handle it," she exclaimed, standing up. "I know you won't say a word to Richard about this."

"I can't make any promises. He's my brother. If he comes to me, I won't tell him, but I'll send him to you."

Dawn wanted to stay and argue with Zack, but she let it go. Now wasn't the time to battle Zack over this. She had to find a way to keep Johnny's mouth shut for good. "Fine. I'll deal with Richard when the time comes. Johnny is my main problem now, and I'm going to make sure he isn't much longer."

Chapter Thirty-One

"I can't believe how fast David Cody got the two buildings connected to each other." Zack's steps slowed as he got a good look at the new section of *D4* that was part dance floor and lounge. Dawn had really outdone herself with the floor designs on the place. Richard would be a fool to let Dawn leave him in a few weeks, but after the secret Dawn let him in on, he wasn't quite sure what his brother's reaction might be.

"Dawn is a world-class manager. She's almost too smart for that title. I'm thinking about making her my partner," Richard tossed out.

"Are you talking about marriage or the restaurant?"

"Both, if Dawn will stay still long enough for me to ask her." Richard spoke in a voice filled with love and respect for the woman he cared about.

"You really do love her, don't you?"

"Yes, I do, but I'm having the hardest time making Dawn believe me. She thinks I'm in love with the way she helped me pulled *D4* out of the ruins. I told her I was in love with her weeks ago, and ever since then, she has been avoiding me. I think I might be losing her, and there's nothing I can do about it."

The last couple of words came out mumbled as Richard tried to conceal his emotions.

Running his hands down his face, Richard got himself back under control. He didn't want to break down in front of his brother. "Was it this hard for you to make Traci believe you loved her?"

Zack patted him on the back. "I had to convince Traci and Cherise both about how much I adored Traci. I almost lost her, and it nearly killed me. Don't make the same mistakes I did. Listen to Dawn when she wants to talk to you. She's a very special woman, but if you don't stop having Brad follow her, she's going to leave you."

"Brad and his big mouth! When did you find out about it?"

"He told me and Lee over our weekly dinner the other night. Even Lee thinks it wrong, which is surprising with the way he's always following Cherise around," Zack lectured.

"Tell me a different way to do it, then. You have your gorgeous wife and adorable son. Let me in on how to get mine."

"Communication," Zack answered. "Dawn isn't a section of the restaurant you're trying to run. She's a living, breathing woman that only wants your love and attention. She wants to be able to feel safe with you and trust you with her fears."

* * * *

He didn't understand where Zack was coming from with this. He would be in Dawn's corner any time she was in trouble. "Dawn doesn't have any fears. She's one of the strongest women that I know."

"Are you sure about that? You're having Brad follow her for a reason."

"Will you stop tossing that in my face?"

"Tell Brad to stop, and I will, but until you do, I'm going to remind you of it every day. Dawn already has enough trouble from Johnny without you adding to her problems," Zack snapped at Richard.

Richard saw the look of shock that passed across his brother's features. Why did Zack know about some guy named Johnny bothering Dawn and he didn't? Had she been confiding in his older brother instead of him?

"Who in the hell is Johnny, and what is he doing to Dawn?"

Zack hurried from the room, not stopping to explain or answer Richard's question. His brother picked up his briefcase and then moved toward the door. Richard wasn't about to let Zack leave without answering at least one of his questions.

"Don't act like you didn't hear me. Why do you know about this guy and I don't? What is he doing to Dawn? Is she in some kind of danger? Damn it, Zack, answer me," Richard hollered at his brother's back.

Zack stopped at the entranceway to D4, but he didn't look at him. "When Dawn comes to you, don't judge her or place the blame on her. What happened wasn't her fault or yours, but you need to be understanding." With those words left hanging in the air, Zack pushed open the doors to D4 and left.

Richard replayed Zack's words in his head over and over, but he wasn't making any sense of them. Why would Dawn need him not to place blame on her? What was going on? Was she sleeping with this

237

Johnny guy, and she didn't know how to tell him? He wanted answers, and there was only one way to find out.

Half an hour later, Richard sat inside his car, parked three houses away from Dawn's house. She had told him last night that she had another lunch date today and would meet up with him later. Well, it was about time he found out who was so important. Brad's surveillance of her didn't work out, so he was taking over. He would do it right and get all the information he sought.

Chapter Thirty-Two

Dawn twisted her fingers until she thought she was going to break them at the knuckles. Johnny was late, and it scared the hell out of her. When it came to getting money for his addiction, Johnny was right on time. Undoing her hands, Dawn shuffled over to the window, pushed the curtain aside and peeked outside. Where in the hell was Johnny?

He had called her about eight times over the past week, wanting more money, and she finally found a way to get it, and now his skinny ass wasn't even here on time to collect it. This was the last time he was going to guilt trip her for more money. In addition, his little blackmail scheme was over, and the Bank of Dawn was closed.

Johnny couldn't be her whole focus, not when *D4* was opening back up in less than two weeks. All the new tables and chairs arrived last week, along with the rough draft of the menu. Richard told her that he was bringing back the same chef and a handful of the male servers. He promised her that none of the old hostesses were coming back, and she was thrilled about that.

Without a doubt, Richard was going to need an effective support staff for *D4* after she was gone. He couldn't start playing favorites with anyone like he did last time, or *D4* would be back in trouble in a matter of days.

Running her fingers through her hair, Dawn massaged her scalp as she roamed around the room. "What am I going to do without Richard?" She had gotten used to the routine of getting up early in the morning and seeing his handsome face in the bed beside her. "You promised yourself that you wouldn't get attached to him," she scolded herself. Now look what happened; you've fallen deeper in love with him."

Dawn tried to convince herself that leaving Richard wouldn't take a piece of her heart, but she couldn't. Richard Drace was in her blood, and nothing was ever going to get him out. "Okay, you have to stop thinking about Richard and get it back on Johnny." As the minutes ticked by, the more concerned she became something was wrong. Johnny didn't have anyone else to blackmail for money, so where in the hell was his narrow behind at?

* * * *

"Man, get your hands off of me. I don't have to get treated like a criminal." Johnny jerked his arm away from the man that literally snatched him off the street.

"Sit your ass down in the seat, and I won't treat you like one," Richard snapped. He almost hadn't caught Johnny in time before he made it to Dawn's porch. Looking at the man, he saw all the signs of a drug user in front of him. What reason did the lowlife have to be around Dawn?

Johnny flopped down in a chair at the outside of *D4*. "I don't know what you want with me."

"Stop lying. You know good and well the reason you're with me. Now you're going to tell me the reason Dawn has been paying you money."

"I don't know who or what you're taking about," Johnny blatantly lied.

"Listen. Either you tell me what is going on, or I'll call the cops." Richard wanted nothing more than to beat this guy until his eyes rolled in the back of his head, but he wouldn't because he wasn't going to use violence. If this jerk wanted more money, then it would come from him, not Dawn.

"I wouldn't do that if I was you," Johnny sneered. Reaching inside his denim jacket, his sullied fingers pulled something out. "Unless you want them to acquire a copy of this tasty videotape I have on Dawny."

An unbearable pain shot its way right to the center of his heart as Richard stared at the tape that Johnny was teasing him with. How did he know Dawn was even on that thing? He could be trying to play him for a fool. "Why should I believe a word coming out of your mouth? You could be lying to me."

"You think so?" Johnny taunted, waving the tape in his face.

"Yes, drug addicts aren't known for their honesty."

Johnny stopped waving the tape as his eyes took on an unearthly glow. "Don't you dare act like you're better than me. If it wasn't for you, Dawn wouldn't have made this baby here," Johnny muttered, tapping the side of his leg with the tape. "You and only you made her do the things on here."

Knocking the video away from him, Richard hated that he was starting to believe Johnny. Dawn met this creep every day for weeks, trying to keep this from him, and now he possessed the ability to make the tape and Johnny both disappear. He didn't have to think twice about his decision. "I have two questions for you."

"What are they?"

"How do I know that's the only copy of the tape and how much will it take for you to give up that thing and leave Dawn alone? I mean, disappear like you had never been born?" Richard calculated how money he still had left from Zack's check in the bank. He hoped that it was enough for the person sitting beside him.

"Now we are on the same page." Johnny grinned at him, displaying a row of yellowed teeth. "How much do you think Dawn's dignity is worth?"

Chapter Thirty-Three

The remote landed somewhere between the table and the front door after Richard finished viewing the videotape he got from Johnny. How could Dawn not tell him about this? Hell, he asked her time and time again if she needed his help, but she told him no. The images were fried into his long-term memory, making it almost impossible to see Dawn in the same light as he used to.

Out of all the jobs she could have given her attention, the Pleasure Pal was the place she decided on. He wasn't going to take the blame for this. She made a conscious decision to let those guys touch her like that. Shit, the disgust he felt for her now was off the charts. He couldn't handle this on his own. Picking up the phone, he dialed the numbers of the three men who he knew wouldn't judge without hearing the whole story.

* * * *

Thirty minutes later, Richard clicked off the television, faced the men sitting across from him and tried gauging their reactions, but he couldn't read their faces. "The floor is open. What should I do about Dawn?" In his heart, the decision had already been made, but he still wanted to hear the advice of his brothers.

"Do you really have to ask that?" Lee exclaimed.

"Yeah, I thought you would know what to do," Zack interjected.

"Even I know what choice I would make, too," Brad added.

"Get rid of the tape, and never tell Dawn you saw it," the trio answered.

"That happened when you weren't with her, so it doesn't concern you. If I found out about something from Traci's past, it wouldn't kept me from marrying her. I loved her and wanted to be with her," said Zack.

"After seeing the tape, did the love you have for Dawn die?" Lee questioned. "Because if it did, maybe you weren't in love with her in the first place. I heard that Hamilton Madsen had a thing for her."

"Hamilton better stay away from Dawn, if he knows what's good for him," Richard said.

"Why? Aren't you planning on dumping her anyway after *D4* reopens?" Brad froze in his seat as Richard's hard gaze landed on him.

"Why don't you stop giving me advice about my life, and deal with Alicia and her feelings for Max? Didn't you see how good they look together in that newspaper article yesterday?"

"That was low, even for you, Richard." Brad got up from the couch and then stormed out before he could stop him.

"Wonderful," Richard muttered, watching the door close behind his youngest brother. "I've pissed him off." He had had no intention of saying that to Brad when he invited him over. "I'll call him later to apologize."

"I love Brad, but he can wait. Are you going to tell Dawn or not?" Lee questioned, regaining his attention. "I vote that you don't. She might not want to relive the Pleasure Pal."

"Don't listen to that idiot over there." Zack waved his finger in the direction of the oldest Drace brother. "After the celebration for D4 is over, take Dawn to the side and get all of it out in the open. Never start a relationship out on a lie."

"She lied to me," Richard said. "Was it okay for her to do it to me?"

Zack's mouth dipped into a deep frown at his question. "I don't know how Dawn lied to you, but I don't have time to stay and find out. I have a date tonight with a very sexy woman." Standing up, Zack patted him on the shoulder. "Don't listen to Lee. Tell Dawn and it won't bite you in the ass later." His brother gave him a crooked smile and then was gone before he could reply.

Groaning, he fell down on the couch next to Lee and closed his eyes. "You still think I need to act like I know nothing?"

"Hey, it's not my decision to make. It's all left up to you. Are you willing to lie to keep her or tell the truth and lose her?"

* * * *

"Have you been busy, or are you hiding from me?"

Dawn placed the menu back on the table as the sexy drawl of Richard's voice skimmed over her body. She hadn't had any extra time to spend around him outside the restaurant because of the last-minute details. All of her hard work came down to tonight and this reopening. She prayed it was everything that Richard visualized that day at the park, when he offered her the old job back. She couldn't believe this would be the last time she got to see his handsome face or hear the stirring sound of his voice.

"You know that I've been working like a dog to get Jeff Masters to come and review the improved *D4*," she answered, turning to look at the man she loved. "I called you a couple of times, but you didn't return my messages."

"I'm sorry, Kitten. Brad is going through some things, and I spent a couple of days at his home," Richard answered, drawing her into his arms. "Have I mentioned how tasty you look in that dress? I spotted you the second I came through the kitchen."

"Why did you come through the kitchen?" She leaned back in Richard's arms to get a better look at his face. "Is there something wrong with the front door? We open in five minutes," she panicked. "Do I need to call a locksmith or something?" Dawn moved to get out of Richard's arms, but he pressed her back to his chest.

"No, everything is wonderful. There's a line of people down the block to get in here, and I have you to thank for that. You made *D4* better than it used to be." Placing a kiss on her forehead, Richard's strong fingers roamed over her back.

"The success of *D4* will come from both of us. Neither one of us did more work that the other. I couldn't have purchased most of the things I did without the generosity of your brothers," Dawn said. "You showed me I still have what it takes to run a restaurant smoothly."

Richard moved back from her, and then a calloused finger traced her bottom lip, sending tiny shivers all over her body. "Don't you know that I'll do anything for you? Battle any demon you might have, slay any dragon that is threatening you, pay off anyone that holding a secret over you."

Pay off anyone that is holding a secret over me? Oh, God, Richard knows about Johnny!

Twisting her head away, she stepped back until at least five feet separated her from Richard. Then she asked him the question she feared the most. "You know about Johnny, don't you?"

Chapter Thirty-Four

Shit! Why did he have to open his big mouth? Lee told him to keep quiet and he didn't listen. "Dawn, don't get upset with me. I can explain everything," Richard pleaded as Dawn continued to move back from him. "You don't have to worry about Johnny any more. I took care of him. We don't have that much money left in petty cash, but it doesn't matter."

"How could you know about Johnny? I never…never mentioned him to you," Dawn muttered. "Tell me, how did you find out about my ex?"

Richard swallowed hard as a deep dread settled in the middle of his chest, where his heart used to be. He couldn't tell her. Dawn would freak out on him. Damn, why did he ever let Brad follow her in the first place? Impulse…yeah, he would blame it on impulse, but now wasn't the time to drag all of this out. *D4* was just about to reopen its doors in a few minutes, after being closed for close to four months.

"Kitten, we don't have the time to go into this now. But I swear to you, I don't think of you any differently after seeing the tape."

"You watched the…tape?" Dawn whispered, as tears gathered in the back of her eyes. "Please, God, tell me you didn't show it to your brothers, too? I know how close the four of you are."

He didn't want Dawn freaking out on one of the most important days in their lives. "I don't want to go into this now. Will you please meet me in our office after I get done with the interview?"

"No, we have enough time to tell me how you found out about Johnny," she snapped.

"Please drop it," Richard pleaded. "I don't want us fighting, especially not tonight."

"Fine, if you don't want to tell me, then I'll ask one of your brothers," she threatened. "I know I saw them in the lounge." Dawn turned to leave, but Richard stopped her.

"I had Brad following you. He saw you arguing with Johnny, then came back and told me. Weeks later, I parked a couple of house down from yours and snatched Johnny before he could knock on your door."

"You had Brad tracking me like I was a deer in the forest?" Dawn accused. "You couldn't just come out and ask me about Johnny?"

"I did ask you, and you told me to mind my own business."

"Why didn't you listen?" Dawn asked, as the tears started to cascade down her cheeks. "Johnny was my problem, not yours. I was getting rid of him at my own speed."

"Kitten, I'm in love with you. I wanted to help you. I gave Johnny the money he wanted, then got him a plane ticket back to your hometown. He isn't going to be bothering you any more."

* * * *

"Johnny's gone?"

"Yes, and I told him in no uncertain terms that he was never to contact you again for anything," Richard said, sounding pleased with himself.

Dawn wanted to be exultant Johnny was out of her life, but the way it happened put a sour taste in her mouth. Did Richard honestly think she was fine with this? Not only had he seen the tape, but he showed the thing to his brothers, too. How could she ever be in the same room with them again? Zack already knew about the tape because she decided to tell him. Lee and Brad found out because Richard brought them into her business.

"I can't do this with you." She wasn't about to do anything with him ever again after tonight. "I'm going to check on the staff and make sure everything is set up." Dawn hurried from the room at the exact time the other three Drace brothers came through the opposite door.

* * * *

"Who lit a fire under her pot?" Lee asked Richard as he stared at a fleeing Dawn. "I wanted to tell her how wonderful the place looks. I would have never known it was the same place."

"I let it slip about Johnny," Richard groaned as his heart started to break. Dawn wasn't going to stay with D4 after tonight. He blew up any chances of them ever being together. Damn Zack and his honesty.

"Let her calm down, and she'll be back," Zack chimed in. "Traci forgave me for that Eva incident, and it wasn't even my fault."

"It's not the same thing," Richard snapped, tired of Zack's laid-back attitude since he married Traci. "You didn't have someone following her, and you didn't pay off an ex-boyfriend for a tape of her at a sex club."

"Dawn didn't have sex with any of those guys. We all saw what was on that tape. It was more like a prolonged foreplay session than anything else." Brad's voice butted in hoping to defuse the situation. "Hell, I wouldn't dump Alicia for something that happened when we weren't together."

Richard pulled out a chair at the table and waited for his brothers to join him. "I'm not dumping Dawn. I had other plans for her tonight."

"What sort of plans?" Lee asked.

Richard shrugged his shoulders and then drummed his fingers across the linen tablecloth. "It doesn't matter now. Dawn is through with me."

"Don't think like that. Give her time to absorb everything, and she'll be back," Brad encouraged. "She loves you."

"She used to love me. I have ruined any chances of us being together." He believed in the impossible, but he wasn't a believer in not seeing what was right in his face. "Thanks for talking with me, guys, but I need to head to the front. It's almost time to open the doors." Richard got up and left the room, leaving his brothers confused and concerned about his future with Dawn.

* * * *

Pausing outside his closed office door, Richard rested his head against it. He wanted more than anything for Dawn to be waiting for him on the other side, but she wouldn't be. Every time he tried to get her alone tonight, she found a way to bring another person into the conversation or just walked away from him.

Things didn't get any better when Emily showed up wearing a black dress that practically looked like a nightgown and wrapped herself around his arm for most of the night. It had taken both Lee and Zack to finally get her out the front door.

Pushing open the door, he strolled over to his desk and collapsed down in the chair, wondering where Dawn was if she wasn't with him. Could he have messed things up any worse than they already were? Dawn told him not to meddle in her personal life, but being the man he was, he didn't listen. Now his stubbornness had cost him his soulmate, and he was out of apologies.

No, it wasn't going to be this way. His heart refused to believe what his mind told him. Dawn Summers wasn't out of his life. She would be his, if he had to camp outside on her doorstep. All the nights he spent watching her inside his home were far from over.

He spun his chair around to his computer and was about to click on his email icon, when he noticed a note taped to the monitor. His fingers ripped off the familiar pink note card, bearing Dawn's perfect handwriting.

Richard,
The reopening of D4 was an amazing success. Jeff Masters loved you and told me he would tell all of his

friends about you. Thank you so much for rehiring me and making me a part of your dream again.

My contract to you is fulfilled, and I'm no longer an employee at D4. My letter of resignation is inside your desk, along with a check for what I think you paid Johnny for the tape.

I'll never forget our time together. It was the best few months of my life.

Oh, by the way, I don't want you worrying about me finding another job. I'm working for Hamilton at his restaurant, and the pay is everything I ever wanted.

Take care, and keep those crazy brothers in line.

Dawn

Richard balled up the ridiculous note and flung it into the trashcan by his desk. "Oh, Kitten, if you think things are over between us, then you're going to be blown out of Hamilton's expensive office."

Chapter Thirty-Five

"You look very cute sitting behind Hamilton's desk, but you aren't going to be there much longer."

Dawn dropped her pen on the report she was working on, raised her eyes, and found Richard lounging in the open doorway. He had no idea how sensuous his voice sounded to her after not hearing it for a week. She quickly calmed her nerves, so he wouldn't know her true emotions.

"Mr. Drace, what a nice surprise. Is there something that I can do for you?" She tried to ignore how Richard's eyes grew hard at her formal use of his name.

"Yes, you can drop that Mister crap and give me a kiss. I know you want to," he murmured, sauntering into the room.

"This isn't the time or place for your flirting, Richard," Dawn replied, calling her former boss and the love of her life by his first name. "Hamilton is expecting me to meet him for an early dinner."

"Sorry, but that dinner got cancelled." Richard smirked. "He got called back home on an emergency. He'll probably be out of the country for a while."

"What did you do?" Dawn leaped up from her seat. "I need this job and sending my boss on a wild goose chase isn't going to help me keep it."

"I only ordered a few extra cases of wine, and they needed his approval to send them." Richard grinned and came around the desk to stand in front of her. "Do you know how much you broke my heart by leaving?"

Stay cool. Don't let his charisma sway you.

"My time with *D4* was over, so I moved on. As a business man, you should understand why I left."

"Sure…but as a boyfriend, I want to drag you back to my house, out of Hamilton's reach." Richard ran his fingers along her collarbone, making her knees melt. "I almost called you countless times, but I waited."

"Why?" she asked, leaning into his touch. This man had her heart.

"Wanted to give you time to get over the Johnny thing."

She tried to move back, but Richard laid his hand on her shoulder. "Don't run from me again."

"Why should I stay? What could you possibly say to make me not want to leave?"

Tightening his hold, Richard stared at her, and then a soft and loving smile touched his firm lips. "I can't let you leave me because you gave my first taste of love, and I'm not about to give that up. You made me see that I can have the same relationship Zack has with Traci."

She gloried briefly at Richard's words until something hit her. "The Pleasure Pal will always be a part of my past. Can you handle that?"

Kissing her, Richard wrapped her in her arms. "Kitten, I forgot about that tape the same day I saw it, and so should you. If I blame you for that, then I have to shoulder equal blame for sending you there with my words. I love you more than anything in this world. I would have signed over *D4* to Johnny to find out what he held over you. Will you marry me?"

"If I say yes, I guess I'll have to give up my new job?" she teased, already knowing the answer.

"Damn right it does." The drawl she loved so much breathed by her ear.

"Well, you better give me another kiss, so I can get a list started for Hamilton to look over when he gets back into town," Dawn exclaimed before Richard covered her waiting mouth with his.

About the Author

Marie Rochelle is an award-winning author of erotic, interracial romance, including the Phaze titles *All the Fixin'*, *My Deepest Love: Zack*, and *Caught*.. Visit her online at http://www.freewebs.com/irwriter/.

EPIC's EPPIE AWARDS

WINNER
Best Erotica 2007
fine flickering hungers
Alessia Brio

FINALIST
Best Poetry 2008
Phaze in Verse
Kally Jo Surbeck, editor

FINALIST
Best Erotica 2008
Coming Together: For the Cure
Alessia Brio, editor

FINALIST
Best GLBT 2008
Phaze Fantasies III
James Buchanan, Jade Falconer,
Eliza Gayle, Jamie Hill,
Selah March, Yeva Wiest

www.EPICAUTHORS.com